Nobody knew if this was exercise, reconnaissance, a religious ritual, or whatever. But they just marched in a straight line for fifteen minutes, turned around, and marched back. They never stopped, never changed direction, never looked to the left or right. All Sharon had to do was get out of their way.

She scurried to one side, then cautiously turned and looked back.

The aliens marched past her like soldiers on parade. Just as the other humans had all said, they ignored her utterly. Sharon started to breathe normally.

Until, suddenly, the line of Panurish stopped and looked at her.

Sharon froze. This wasn't supposed to happen! And then something even weirder occurred: the Panurish all bent toward her, like they were bowing. But it wasn't a bow. They bent over and each one fixed its third eye, the one on the top of their heads, directly on Sharon.

She was so frightened it took her a minute to realize that the Panurish *weren't* actually looking at her.

They were looking at Tara.

The baby was delighted. She wanted to crawl toward the interesting people who were looking at her.

Sharon clutched the baby hard and ran. She was afraid to look back over her shoulder. How could Sharon outrun them, the camp was so far away, she was panting already . . .

Coming Soon in
DAVID BRIN'S OUT OF TIME *series*
from Avon Books

TIGER IN THE SKY
by Sheila Finch

THE GAME OF WORLDS
by Roger MacBride Allen

DAVID BRIN'S
OUT OF TIME
YANKED!

NANCY KRESS

CREATED BY DAVID BRIN

AVON BOOKS  NEW YORK

AVON BOOKS, INC.
1350 Avenue of the Americas
New York, New York 10019

Copyright © 1999 by Nancy Kress
"Out of Time" is a trademark of David Brin
Library of Congress Catalog Card Number: 98-94859
ISBN: 0-380-79968-5
www.avonbooks.com

First Avon Books Printing: June 1999

AVON BOOKS TRADEMARK REG. U.S. PAT. OFF. AND IN OTHER COUNTRIES, MARCA REGISTRADA, HECHO EN U.S.A.

Printed in the U.S.A.

WCD   10 9 8 7 6 5 4 3 2 1

For Elizabeth Rose and Victoria Jane,
adventurers of the twenty-first century

J ason Ramsay strolled out of the front door of Benjamin Franklin High liked he owned the place. Well, why not? He did! He'd made the reverse dunk that won the game! That and the sweet three-point play where Wayne fed him the ball . . . Him and Wayne and Clayton and Tyrone, they worked together great. His buds.

.On the sidewalk in front of Franklin, dozens of kids waited for buses. Others walked toward the subways. This was a bad section of New York, everybody said, but Jason thought it was all right. You just had to be careful. Don't get tangled with the gangs, or the drug dealers. Keep your nose clean and your grades high enough to play sports. Watch yourself, and this place wasn't bad at all.

All the hottest babes waved to him, waiting for their buses or heading toward the subway. Tomorrow night he had a date with Mary Ann Jamison, who not only had a bod to make you faint but was a nice girl, too, sweet and fun.

"Hey, Jason, wait," called out Coach Patterson, striding toward him down the sidewalk. Jason grinned.

"Hey, Coach. How you doin'?"

"Got a minute?"

"Sure." He waved at Brandy Nielsen, climbing onto her bus. She was almost as hot as Mary Ann. Brandy waved back and blushed.

"I think we have a problem, Jason."

Problem? Jason didn't see any problem. "Yeah? What's that?"

"You were slacking off out there today."

Slacking *off*? He'd won the game! Didn't Coach notice? But all Jason said aloud was, "We did all right."

"Yes, *we* did. Because your teammates made you look good when you were coasting, and then you got lucky on that final throw. But you weren't giving it your all on that court. I know it and you know it."

Jason said nothing.

"You want to go pro eventually, don't you? NBA?"

"You got it," Jason said. He *was* going to go pro. He was going to be great.

The coach sighed. "You know how many kids have that dream, Jason? Thousands. Maybe millions. Now, I'm not saying you aren't talented. You are. And you have something else a lot of hopefuls don't. You can pull together a group of kids so they work like a team. You're a natural leader. But for the NBA, that isn't enough."

Jason didn't like this conversation. Another bus pulled away and he waved at Lateesha Stevens. Another hot babe.

"Jason," Coach said patiently, "hear me."

"I'm hearing."

2

"No, you're not. You're listening, but you're not hearing. You need to focus on what you're doing, work harder, stop coasting along on your talent. How many practices you miss this month?"

"Well, you know, a good bud had a birthday, and then my brother, Brian, he . . ."

"No good, Jason. If you're going to do basketball, you got to *do* it. If you're serious."

"I know, Coach. You're right. A hundred percent."

The coach sighed again. Jason wished he'd stop doing that. Coach said, "That's why it's so hard to get through to you, Ramsay. You listen and smile and agree and get everybody on your side, but you don't *hear*."

"I hear you, Coach." Another bus pulled up, the crosstown bus from across the park. Jason watched the babes get off. Maybe Brian would get off, too. He sometimes took this bus home from work.

"I give up," Coach Patterson said. "You need something to shock you into focus, but I don't know what it would take for you to really start caring about something. Meanwhile, just don't miss any more practices!"

"Absolutely not," Jason said. "I'll be at every one!" Coach strode away, shaking his head. He got so worked up about everything, Jason thought. Coach was a great guy, but he didn't understand about getting along, getting over, enjoying what flowed by.

Brian wasn't on the bus after all. Well, he'd see his brother at home. Whistling, Jason started north along Amsterdam Avenue.

At Ninety-sixth Street, he suddenly got thirsty. He turned into a Korean grocer for a Coke. After he paid for it, he lingered by the magazine rack at the back of the store, leafing through the new issue of *Sports Illustrated*.

Something weird was going down by the magazine rack.

An electric blue light seemed to be growing up out of the floor. Jason stared. The light got bigger and bigger and seemed to be spinning. And it hummed, a low sound that Jason felt—rather than heard—in his bones.

What the—

Jason looked around. Nobody else saw; the owner was stacking cans of soup on a shelf and there were no other customers in the store.

The spinning light moved an inch to the right.

"Hey," Jason said—and the light answered him.

"Jason Ramsay," it said, and Jason was so surprised he didn't even jump. His mouth fell open, and he was standing there staring at the eerie blue light when it spun itself into a deep tunnel and sped across the floor under his feet. Jason made a wild grab for the magazine rack, which he caught hard enough to pull over on himself. A sharp metal edge struck his forehead. Everything went dark, and the spinning tunnel sucked him in.

The cheerleaders were back again.

Sharon Myers shrank into her chair in the far back corner of the Spencerville Public Library. She didn't want them to see her. Not that they would talk to her—people hardly ever talked to

Sharon, and she was used to that. But two of the girls, Lindsey and Sue, would give Sharon those mean little smiles that meant *What a dork. Sitting alone in the library every afternoon, reading and reading because nobody likes her.*

Usually Sharon had this part of the library to herself. She liked sitting in the big deep chair in the corner, losing herself in a good book. And certainly it was better than going home. Anything was better than going home.

Today she was researching her project for tech class. The six junior varsity cheerleaders were probably here for the same reason. They weren't in Sharon's class, but all ninth graders had to take Technology & Communication.

She found out she was right when a boy wandered in. Sam Cassidy, from the junior varsity football team.

"Hey, Sam," Lindsey said. She tossed her long blond hair.

"Hey yourself," Sam said. "You doing King Kong's homework?" Mr. Konger was the tech teacher.

"Yes," Sue said. She fluffed her short green-and-white cheerleader skirt. "We're doing a group grope."

All of them laughed. Sharon didn't think it was funny. But she wondered what the cheerleaders were doing. The project was to research and demonstrate some form of communication that computers had made obsolete, or at least less important. But what could six people demonstrate together?

"So what's this group grope look like?" Sam said.

"We'll show you!" Nicole said.

The girls all giggled and protested. "Here?" "Come on, Nicole!" "The librarian will kill us!" But then they started pushing chairs out of the way to clear the floor. Each girl picked up a "flag" made from cutting and pasting pieces of colored paper. The girls lined up in a row and started waving their flags, one after another, holding the papers.

"So what's that?" Sam said, leaning against a bookcase, smiling lazily at them.

"Semaphore!" Sue shouted. "The way ships used to signal to each other! The papers are signal flags!"

"Yeah?" Sam said. "And what are your flags signaling?"

The girls looked at each other and collapsed into laughter, falling on each other's necks and looking sideways at Sam. So the message must be something sexy, Sharon thought. Sam just went on smiling as if he knew what the message was, which Sharon doubted. The librarian, Mrs. Staines, came rushing over.

"Girls! Girls! You can't practice cheers in here! Either use the library for its proper purpose or go outside!"

"Okay, okay," Nicole muttered. When the librarian left, she smirked. "What an old bat. Only likes dorks like Miss Brown Nose Rose-of-Sharon."

So they *had* seen her. Sharon looked down at her book. For the next half hour she didn't move, trying to become invisible. The cheerleaders whispered and giggled, passing reference books back and forth.

When they finally left, Sharon went over to their table. They'd left their books open at the pictures of semaphoring. Sharon worked out the six flag positions they'd shown Sam with the pieces of colored paper. The first two flags, taken together, were a message, and the other four flags spelled out a word. The whole semaphore said, "You should pull as close to me as possible, H-U-N-K."

For a minute, loneliness pierced her. She wished she were the kind of girl who could make jokes with a boy, who had friends, who had the right clothes to wear and the right haircut. . . .

Enough of that. She had things to do. God, it was five-thirty already.

Sharon grabbed her books and hurried out of the library. As she passed the front desk, Mrs. Staines called out pleasantly, "Good night, Rose-of-Sharon."

Sharon nodded back. She'd never had the nerve to tell Mrs. Staines she didn't like her full name.

Outside it was cold. Sharon pulled her coat tighter around her. It was old and thin, a hand-me-down her older sister Johnna had left behind when she moved out. The air felt like snow, which was reasonable for November, and the street lights were already on in the winter dark.

How beautiful Spencerville was in the early evening! The way those black lacy tree branches looked against the sky . . . it could take your breath away. It reminded Sharon of that poem they had read in English class about a Grecian vase, "Beauty is truth, truth beauty . . ." Keats. Sharon had liked that poem. Most of the kids didn't care about things like poetry or trees against the sky. They hated Spencerville, they said, and couldn't wait until they were old enough to get out of school and out of town.

Sharon was different, and she knew it. It made her feel lonely. Not just the differences about liking poetry, but the differences in her home that everybody knew about because that's the way small towns were. Everybody knew that Sharon's father had left town with a woman who worked in the Grain & Feed. Everybody knew that Sharon's mother spent every night getting drunk at the Lamplighter. Everybody knew that Sharon's sister Johnna had dropped out of high school to have a baby and didn't marry her boyfriend, who dumped her, and now Johnna was living with a man everybody said "was old enough to be her father."

Well, things would be different for Sharon. She was going to finish school, go to college. Get a better life than her mother's or Johnna's. Somehow.

Oh, God. Almost six and she hadn't started dinner yet. Her mother would be furious.

But when Sharon burst through the door of the ramshackle little house on Sycamore Street, nobody even mentioned dinner. There was far worse trouble than a missed meal.

Jason opened his eyes and wondered where he was.

"He's awake," a woman said.

A hospital. It had to be a hospital. White room, white blanket, his head hurt . . . But it *wasn't* a hospital. No hospital had a person in it that you could look right through and see the wall behind. He could see *through* the woman standing by his bed! No hospital contained a ghostly person made of light but also three-dimensional, like a transparent sculpture that could move and talk.

"He's awake," the transparent person said, and vanished. A second later a real person who looked exactly like the ghost image walked through a door that didn't open or close. Or maybe she had walked through the wall. *Where the hell am I?* he thought.

"Hello, Jason," the real person—if it was a real person—said. "Don't be frightened. I'm Dr. Serena Mep Cee. Do you have a headache?"

Jason sat up. He did have a headache. But that seemed to him the least of his problems. He took a deep breath, pulled himself together, and smiled. "Yeah, a little headache. How *you* doin'?"

"See?" another voice said in thin air. "I told you. A natural team-builder."

"Quiet, please, da Vinci," Dr. Cee said. "Jason, I'm fine. Thanks for asking. I'm glad you're not frightened. But now you need to prepare yourself for a great shock. You're not in New York, and you're not in 1999. This is the future."

"Yeah, right," Jason said.

"Yes, it is. But before we convince you of that, or tell you any more, I want to say immediately that you will be going home eventually. In fact, you can go home after just one hour, if you like. But for that one hour, you must listen to us explain why we brought you here."

"Explain away," Jason said. He felt light-headed. None of this was happening. It was a hallucination of some kind. Had he been doing a drug? No, he didn't do drugs, he didn't ever do drugs. This wasn't a high, it was some sort of weird dream or something. Over in a minute. Might as well go with the flow until it ended.

"We brought you here to save the future," the woman said.

Jason laughed. Save the future! Man, how cheesy could you get? So it wasn't a dream. It was a practical joke, a really good practical joke. His buds must have spent days dreaming up this one. In a minute Tyrone would walk through the door, and Wayne, and even Brian. . . .

What walked through the door was a robot, another transparent person you could see right through, and another doctor. This one was a man, although he wore the same long white shirt and short pants as the woman. Unlike the woman, he wasn't smiling.

"Hello, Jason," he said. "Welcome to 2336."

Sharon could hear her mother shouting even before she opened the front door to her house. And her mother wasn't sober.

". . . think you can just barge in here like some kind of queen and—"

Sharon went inside. The tiny living room was a mess. Dirty glasses, newspapers, clothing, and in the middle her mother and her older sister, Johnna, yelling at each other.

"—dump your responsibilities on me like—"

"I don't care what you say! I'm going and you and nobody else can't—"

"—the irresponsible brat you always were, you got another think—"

"—stop me! I'm not going to turn out like you, another wasted drunk who—"

The baby, Sharon thought. If Johnna was here, then so was her baby. Little Tara would be scared and upset, listening to her mother and grandmother shout at each other.

"—coming! I did my time with kids and I'm not—"

"—let one mistake wreck her life! If you'd been any kind of mother—"

But where was the baby? There was no diaper bag in the living room, no squeeze toys, no Tara.

"—going to raise yours too!"

"—in the first place, I wouldn't be in this position!"

Sharon hurried into the kitchen. No Tara.

The bathroom. No Tara. There were only the two tiny bedrooms above, hers and her mother's. Then she heard a soft babble.

Tara was on the little glassed-in porch that connected to the kitchen, still dressed in her snowsuit. The porch was jammed full because Johnna had brought all Tara's stuff: Pampers and a portacrib and a cardboard box spilling out baby clothes. In the middle of it all Tara sat in an infant seat she'd really outgrown, smiling and cooing to herself.

Sharon knelt down on the porch floor beside the baby. "Hello, little one."

Tara babbled and held up her arms to be picked up.

At nine months, she was the most beautiful baby Sharon had ever seen, and she didn't say that just because Tara was her niece. The blond hair that on Sharon hung in flat lank clumps, and on Johnna frizzed up, on Tara curled into shining ringlets. Tara had big green eyes and perfect, baby-smelling skin. Sharon adored her.

Now she gathered up Tara in her arms and carried her from the cold porch into the house.

Johnna had left. Sharon's mother stood pouring herself a huge whiskey. "Rose-of-Sharon, do you know what that bitch your sister did? Do you *know*?"

"No, Mom."

"She ran off with that crummy new boyfriend of hers and left Tara with me! For me to raise! Says the only reason she has a baby is because I was such a horrible mother. I was a perfect mother! Wasn't I?"

"Mom—"

12

"*Wasn't* I? Say it!"

"You were a great mother," Sharon said, because if she didn't, this would go on all night.

"Damn right I was! And I will be to Tara, too! I know my responsibilities, even if your sister doesn't! Now, sweetie, go get the baby something to eat, will you? We must have something in the pantry. I'll take over right after I finish this drink."

After she finished the drink, Sharon's mother had another drink. Then she fell asleep on the sofa.

Sharon fed Tara some toast, banana, and scrambled eggs. She gave the baby a bath, dressed her in warm pajamas, and rocked her to sleep. Tara's portacrib just barely fit into Sharon's own room, jammed in between her bed and the battered old dresser.

What was she going to do about the baby?

Because it *was* up to her. She was the one who would have to do something. Her mother would kiss Tara and cry and say how Tara was at home now with her granny, and then her mother would drink too much and pass out. That wasn't safe for a baby. That's why Sharon knew it was up to her.

But how could she go to school and watch Tara, too? For one thing, she had to do more research at the library on her Technology & Communication project. More long-term, she had to finish school. And then find a way to go to college.

But she also had to take care of Tara. It had been bad enough for Johnna and Sharon, growing up in this house. But at least then her father had been here, and her mother hadn't been as bad as she was now. So how was Sharon going to go to school *and* watch Tara? Nobody could be in two places at once. Maybe Johnna would come back.

Maybe she wouldn't.

Sharon fell asleep planning and worrying.

The next morning Sharon went straight to the hallway outside her principal's office. It was a while before Mr. Ruhl noticed she was there.

"Rose-of-Sharon! I didn't see you. Come in, come in."

Sharon sat in a chair across from Mr. Ruhl's desk. She'd read in magazines in the library that principals in big-city schools had to deal with gang fights, drug raids, arson, death threats. But Spencerville was different. Mr. Ruhl's desk was covered with flyers for the Thanksgiving PTA bake sale. What would it be like, Sharon wondered, to have a mother you could go to and say, *I need something for the bake sale, could we make that great chocolate cake again?* Sharon pushed that out of her mind. Concentrate on what has to get done.

"What can I do for you?" Mr. Ruhl said.

"You can let me bring—"

"Speak up, Rose-of-Sharon, I can't hear you."

"You can let me bring my nine-month-old niece to school with me. My sister left her with my mother, who drinks too much to take care of the baby. So I have to."

Mr. Ruhl stared at her. Sharon wondered what she'd said wrong. She'd only spoken the truth. Maybe the words had rushed out a little fast, but they were still the truth.

"Tara can come with me to class, in her infant seat. In lunch and study halls I'll go home with her. I live just a few blocks away."

Mr. Ruhl went on staring.

"Well . . . okay?" Sharon said. She couldn't think what else to say.

"No, I'm sorry, it's not okay," Mr. Ruhl finally said. "This school isn't . . . I know in some big cities they have special programs for unwed mothers to bring their babies to school, not that *you're* an unwed mother of course, but we're just not set up for it here. You must see that, Rose-of-Sharon. And as for going home between classes, there are insurance reasons why no student may leave the premises during school hours. And anyway, your sister's baby is not your problem. Your education must come first."

"I can still get my education," Sharon said quietly. "I can do it."

"I don't think you realize how we . . . It's out of the question, my dear. There are other alternatives."

"Like what?"

"Well, like, for instance, foster care for the child—"

Instantly Sharon stood up. He didn't understand. Tara was her niece . . . *family*. You didn't send family to be cared for by strangers. At least she didn't. The Myerses took care of their own.

"Thank you, Mr. Ruhl." She turned to go.

"Rose-of-Sharon, wait, you must see—"

Sharon didn't see. She didn't have time to see. She had to find daycare for Tara.

Jason had been listening to Dr. Cee and Dr. Orgel for twenty minutes. He sat on the edge of his hospital-bed-only-it-wasn't, his long legs braced on the floor, and tried to get a handle on what was happening. A handle? He'd settle for a tiny touch.

"Okay," Jason said finally, "let me see if I got this all straight. This is the future."

"Yes," Dr. Cee said.

"And I got 'yanked' into it by your time machine, right? You were looking for me specific-like, by name, and you got me?"

"Yes. We yanked you," Dr. Cee said.

"But the . . . the 'yank' didn't cause this cut on my head that knocked me out?"

"Certainly not," Dr. Orgel said impatiently. "Yanking does not cause injury. You hit your head on something in your own time." He was the head of the *Yanks project*, officially known as Operation Hourglass, and he hadn't smiled yet.

Not that it mattered if these dudes smiled or not, Jason thought, because they weren't real. No way. Jason was back at his first theory. This wasn't a practical joke—no chance Brian and Tyrone and Clayton could set up a joke like this. Way too complicated. It was a hallucination. Jason had fallen on his head, or got hit by a fast ball playing pick-up baseball, or maybe got attacked, and now he was lying in a hospital in a coma somewhere and hallucinating all this. And what a hallucination! He'd had no idea his brain was smart enough to imagine all this stuff. To tell the truth, he was pretty impressed with himself. So might as well hang with it and go along for the fun.

"So I got yanked, Dr. Orgel"—always good to use people's names, people liked that—"and you put some little thing in my brain so I can understand your future English."

"Yes," said Dr. Cee eagerly. "And not only English. There's a temporary artificial speech center implanted over your Broca area which works by neural induction. We'll remove it before we return you to your own time."

"Fine, sure, whatever," Jason said. "And the reason you brought me here is to go on a mission only gritty kids can do."

"Kids with grit," Dr. Orgel said, frowning. "To tell the truth, Jason, you don't seem to believe us."

Jason laughed. His hallucinations were telling him he didn't believe in them! God, he was good at dreaming up stuff. And his English teacher had the nerve to say his essays were "wooden." If she could see him now!

"Jason," Dr. Cee said, "this is serious. You see, our time—which to you is 'the future'—is peaceful and happy. Mankind has finally learned how to make a society that works. We've solved the problems of your day: war, pollution, disease, crime. But everything has a price. And after centuries of the good life for everybody, we've lost one human quality: grit."

"Okay," Jason said. "Tell me again just what 'grit' is."

"It's hard to define but easy to spot," Dr. Cee said. "A person with grit doesn't give up. He gets things done. He isn't stopped by hardship. He just keeps going."

"Like the Energizer Bunny." Jason grinned.

"The what?"

"Never mind. How do you know I got this 'grit'?"

"We can't tell you that yet," Dr. Orgel said. "We'll tell you that after the mission is over."

The robot had been silent this whole time. Suddenly it said, quite loudly, "Difficulty with Yank 47." At the same moment another transparent person appeared beside Dr. Cee and said, "Serena! A complication on the Myers yank!"

Jason demanded, "What is that transparent stuff? Is that alive?"

"It's a PP—a 'personal projection.' No, it's not alive. It's like a . . . a picture you can send places that you aren't. To give and send messages."

"Way cool," Jason said. "What's that noise?"

In the next room, someone was screaming. Dr. Orgel vanished through the non-door. Jason looked hard, but he still didn't see it open or close. Dr. Cee said worriedly, "Let's just concentrate on you, for the moment. Stay focused, Jason."

She sounded like Coach Patterson, Jason thought. No matter how far into the future you hallucinated yourself, some things didn't change. Somebody was always on your case.

"You got it," Jason said. "I'm focused. I'm on task. You yank kids from the past to do this mission gig. Why kids? Why not yank adults?"

"We can't," Dr. Cee said. "Only kids can teleport, and yanking is one kind of teleporting. You see—"

The noise in the next room suddenly increased. Yelling, crying . . . Jason would swear he was hearing a baby in there. Well, maybe there was a daycare center for the teleport workers.

"Excuse me," Dr. Cee said, and then she vanished through the wall as well, leaving Jason alone.

He got out of bed. Maybe he'd just try that wall gig for himself. But when he walked into the place the two doctors had gone through, all that happened was that he smacked his head against the wall.

"Your current action may injure your body. Please desist."

Jason spun around. It was the robot—yet *another* person telling him what to do!

But was a robot really a 'person'? Jason decided to find out.

Mrs. Northrup opened her front door and smiled. "Why, Sharon, come in, honey. It's a little chaotic, but you won't mind that, will you?"

Sharon didn't mind. Mrs. Northrup, who lived four doors down Sycamore Street from the

Myerses, had a great house. It always smelled of cookies or bread or stew. The big shabby living room was filled with cheerful furniture, bright toys, and small kids. Mrs. Northrup ran a daycare in her house. At the moment two toddlers watched *Sesame Street*, two preschoolers played with trucks, and an infant clung to Mrs. Northrup's shoulder.

"Would you like a cookie, Sharon? And if you don't mind my asking, why aren't you in school?"

"I want to know if—"

"I'm sorry, child, I can't hear you over Big Bird. You're such a quiet little thing. What did you say?"

"I want to know if you can watch Tara every day while I'm at school."

Mrs. Northrup looked sad. "Tara? What about Johnna?"

"Gone," Sharon said. "Left Tara with my mother. And my mother—"

"Never mind. I know. Oh, dear."

Mrs. Northrup sat down in one of the comfortable flowered chairs. Sharon sat in another. A little boy crawled up to her and held out a toy truck, which Sharon took, smiling at him. Tara would like it here.

"The thing is," Mrs. Northrup began. "Oh, dear, this is embarrassing. Tim just got laid off."

Tim was Mrs. Northrup's husband. Sharon waited.

"I would love to watch Tara for you, she's a wonderful baby. But money is really tight right now, Sharon. You're old enough to understand that. The state only allows me to watch six children in my in-home business here. It's true I only have five just now, but I have to take a sixth that is from a paying family, or I just can't make ends meet for Tim and me."

Sharon nodded slowly. It made sense. She'd been thinking only about Tara, but of course the Northrups would have their own bills to pay. Everybody did.

"How much do you charge, Mrs. Northrup?"

"For a child under one year old, seventy-five dollars a week. I'm sorry, but—"

"No, that's okay," Sharon said. After a minute she stood up. "I have to go now."

"Sharon, I'm so sorry. I really wish I could do it, if only to ease the burden on you. You're so quiet, but you take responsibility for everything, don't you, even—"

"Don't accept a sixth kid yet, okay, Mrs. Northrup? I'll be back."

"I'm sorry," said the strange young man behind the library counter, "but Mrs. Staines left on vacation last night. I'm the temporary librarian."

He was young, in his twenties, and had a beard. Not from around here. Sharon said, "When will Mrs. Staines be back?"

"Two weeks. She's taking her vacation through Thanksgiving."

Two weeks! Sharon couldn't wait even one day. Already it was ten-thirty in the morning, and she'd left Tara alone in the house since seven. Well, not alone, her mother was there. For all the good that would do.

She said, "Then maybe you can help. I'd like—"

"Please speak up."

"I'd like to apply for a job in the library. I can—"

"Oh, I have nothing to do with hiring."

"Just a temporary job, until Mrs. Staines can make it permanent."

"I can't authorize even a temporary job. And anyway, how old are you?"

"Fourteen," Sharon said.

"You can't get working papers in this state until you're fifteen."

"I know but—"

"No 'buts.' And no job." He picked up a pile of overdue notices.

Sharon headed home. Mrs. Staines liked her, and might have bent the rules for her. This guy wouldn't. That was the way it was.

She broke into a run. It had finally started to snow, and she ran through huge white flakes like soft doilies. In her bedroom Tara stood whimpering in the portacrib, her diaper wet. Sharon's mother snored in the next room.

Sharon changed the baby, dressed her, and fed her. Then she put on her coat and Tara's to go out. The baby should have some fresh air, but then what? How was Sharon going to take care of Tara and also have her own life?

There seemed no answer. Despair washed over Sharon. She wouldn't give up, but at the moment there seemed no way out. Oh, if she could just tuck Tara safe into herself and take her everywhere without being bothered by having her. If only Tara could be sort of like a baby kangaroo, safe inside a sac while the

22

mother kangaroo got to go about having a life. . . .

Almost without knowing it, Sharon had buttoned her coat around the baby, so that only the top of Tara's blond head showed under Sharon's chin. The baby giggled; she thought it was a game.

Sharon walked numbly out of the kitchen onto the glassed-in porch. She'd moved all the baby stuff Johnna had left to the upstairs, but the porch was still full of junk: A lawnmower that didn't work. A box of Christmas tree ornaments nobody'd used for two years. An old baseball glove. Two battered folding chairs. And something else.

It spun in the corner, a sort of blue box. No—a blue *light*. How did it get on the porch? As Sharon stared, the light began to deepen and spin, until it turned into a tunnel leading sharply downward. And then the tunnel moved from the corner of the porch toward Sharon.

"Sharon Myers," the thing said.

Sharon took a step backward. She had just started to turn to run when the blue tunnel spun under her feet, and time stopped.

4

Jason studied the robot. The weird-looking thing was shaped like a giant tin can with flexible plastic tentacles for arms, a basketball round head, and a screen in its belly. It floated a foot above the floor.

"Hey, robot, how you doin'?"

"Fine, thank you."

"You got a name?"

"Da Vinci," the robot said.

"That's cool. Like the old-time painter, right? The *Mona Lisa*? Babe with the smile?"

"The painting's actual name was *La Gioconda*."

"Whatever," Jason said. The robot seemed smart. Maybe it could help him understand what kind of tricks his brain was playing. "So anyway, Dr. Cee was saying only kids can teleport? That so?"

"Yes," da Vinci said. "It is true."

"What happens if adults teleport?"

"If adults teleport a short distance only once a day or so, they are not affected. If adults teleport longer distances on Earth, or more often than once a day, they get severe, disabling headaches. If they teleport interplanetary, they may die. If they teleport interstellar, through a sally port, they will almost surely die. This is true of both humans and of alien races, except the Devlin."

Alien races? *Alien?* This future he himself had dreamed up in his in-a-coma head had aliens in it? Damn, he was good!

"I'm revved," Jason told the robot. "So only kids can go to other planets outside the solar system, through those . . . what'd you call them?"

"Sally ports," da Vinci said.

"Yeah, sally ports. Only kids can colonize other planets, then? No adults? No school, no homework, no trigonometry?"

"Only children whose brain nerves are still growing may t-port through a sally port and emerge alive. This is because t-porting requires flexibility of the myelin sheath that wraps around the brain. Myelin sheaths do not finish growing until the late teens, which means that the cutoff point for humans t-porting across space is around seventeen years old, give or take a few months."

Jason sat back down on the edge of his bed and smiled at the robot. "Guess you know a lot, huh?"

"I am fully programmed as a library resource, plus special procedures for Project Jason Step Three."

"Yeah? That's 'Jason' like in me?"

"The reference is to you, Jason Ramsay."

"And what's the step three I'm going to be taking?"

"Not *your* third step," the robot said. "The third step for mankind. The mission you're going on with Sharon, Robbie, Jofrid, and Sor. To find the lost colony of the planet Jump."

Jason opened his mouth, then closed it again. Sharon? Robbie? Jofrid? Sor? He didn't know anybody with those names. And no planet Jump, either. And nothing about "t-porting" or "sally ports." In fact, none of this was stuff his brain ever thought about, so how could he have dreamed it up in a coma? What his brain thought about was basketball, and football, and hot babes, and his buds, and food. Not this stuff.

A horrible cold feeling started to creep up Jason's spine.

He said slowly to the robot, "Da Vinci, this is all real, isn't it? I'm not dreaming you. I'm really here in the future? And I'm really going to be sent on a mission to another planet?"

"Only if you choose to go. No young person will ever be sent into danger against his or her will. And no young person would ever be sent at all if adults could accomplish interstellar t-porting. But they cannot. Still, you most definitely have a choice about going on the mission."

"Sure, fine. But the mission is real? You're real? I'm really here in the future?"

"Oh, yes," da Vinci said. "In your future. In 2336. You're really here."

Before Jason could answer, the door opened—or whatever it did—and four people came through. Dr. Cee. Dr. Orgel. Another adult in the same white doctor-clothes. And a girl who looked like she came from his own time. Maybe fourteen, maybe fifteen. Not a babe. Not even a babe-in-training. Skinny, with dirty blond hair, dressed in an old winter coat and Kmart-type sneakers. And yelling.

No. The girl wasn't yelling. She had one of those calm, pale, plain faces that are so hard to remember. And there weren't four people, there were five. Tucked inside the girl's coat, yelling its head off, was a baby.

"I do understand, Dr. Cee," the girl said. She sort of mumbled; Jason had trouble making out her words. "But we're not going back to 1999. Not until the librarian, Mrs. Staines, returns from her vacation and can give me a job. That's two weeks from now."

"But, Sharon—" Dr. Cee began.

Sharon. That was one of the names that da Vinci gave him. Five kids on the mission to the planet Jump: Jason, Sharon, Robbie, Jofrid, Sor. The mission called Project Jason Step Three—*his* mission. Named after him, the "natural team builder." His mission!

"No," he said, louder than he intended. Everybody turned to look at him. Even the baby stopped yelling. "No, no, and more no. We have a mistake here, folks. If I'm leading a mission to the lost colony on Jump, there's no babies going along. No babies at all. Sharon can go, if that's the play, but no babies. That baby stays right here."

"Well, of course," Dr. Cee said. She looked relieved. Dr. Orgel didn't exactly smile, but he frowned a little bit less. Jason relaxed. They were on his side. No baby.

"Little Tara was yanked by mistake," Dr. Cee

told Jason. "The computer that does the yanking can distinguish the right person in the past, but the machinery brings through the t-port anything that seems merged with the Yank. That includes anything the person is holding, but—"

"You ever get a dog that way?" Jason asked with interest. "Or a cat?"

"Yes," da Vinci said, ever ready to supply information. "One cat from 1997, and one temple snake from 1067."

"A *snake*? From 1067? You mean you—?"

"We're getting off the subject," Dr. Orgel said, frowning again. "The point is that Tara was under Sharon's coat and was inadvertently yanked. Sharon, we'll send you and Tara back right now and find another team member for the mission."

"No," Sharon said.

"Yes," Jason said. "No baby on my mission. No way. I don't even *like* babies. No."

Dr. Cee said firmly, "I'm sure there's a way that Sharon can remain with us. The baby will stay here, on Edge Station One, and we will look after her for you, Sharon, while you're on Jason's team. We can do that quite well. Let me show you."

Dr. Cee waved her hand at the wall, and it became a TV screen, or maybe a window—the images were so clear that Jason couldn't tell if they were indeed images, or reality. He saw a park filled with trees, grass, wonderful play equipment. A child climbed on a jungle gym that kept changing shape even as she climbed. A little boy talked to a computer screen, which talked back. An infant crawled toward a bright toy. Beside each child stood a robot like da Vinci, only with more arms. As Jason watched, one robot caught the small falling climber, another helped the boy with his computer, a third picked up a baby and rocked it gently.

"Tara will have everything she needs," Dr. Cee said. "We devote our very best minds to the care and teaching of our young—after all, they're our future. So, Sharon, *your* choice is now this: Do you want to go on the mission and leave Tara here, or would you prefer we return both of you to 1999 right now?"

There was a long, tense pause.

Finally Sharon said, "I'll go on the mission and leave Tara with you."

Dr. Cee looked at her keenly. "And why do you choose that, Sharon? Please speak up."

Sharon said. "If I go on the mission, it will leave me more time to think about what to do about Tara when I do go home."

Jason nodded. Well, fine. He didn't care why the skinny girl left the baby behind, so long as she did. Though, come to think of it, she backed off kind of quick. Weren't people supposed to be chosen for this team because they had "grit"?

He looked suspiciously at Sharon, but she was gazing down at the floor, unbuttoning her coat to take the baby out of it. Tara had a dirty diaper; Jason could smell it from here. What was the deal, was the girl an unwed mother? A big sister? Not that it mattered to Jason. Just so long as he didn't have to have anything to do with this baby. Or any other.

"Dr. Cee," da Vinci said, "the other three team

members of Project Jason Step Three have arrived and been oriented. They're ready to meet Sharon and Jason."

Sharon followed the tall black boy and the two doctors out of the room. At the doorway, the robot held out its long plastic tentacles. It was a moment before Sharon realized that the machine wanted her to hand over Tara.

Sharon clutched Tara. Yes, she'd seen that wonderful daycare center on the TV—but that was *TV*. You saw all kinds of things on television that weren't true.

"Sharon, let da Vinci have the baby," Dr. Cee said.

"Now? So soon?"

"Now. Tara will be fine."

Still Sharon hesitated. The robot—"da Vinci"—reached out a tentacle and put it over Tara's eyes, then took it away, then put it back and "hid" behind Sharon. Tara pulled the tentacle away, squirmed around until she saw da Vinci, and giggled. The robot played the game again, and Tara held out her arms to it.

Sharon said, "Does it have any diapers?"

"It can have the synthesizer . . . Yes. It has diapers."

Sharon let the robot take Tara.

To tell the truth, it felt good to have Tara out of her arms. A baby could be so heavy. And changing a messy diaper was not fun. Besides, since they were going to be here, in the future, until Mrs. Staines came back from vacation, Sharon should see what the future was like. She'd read so many books about the past, for history class, but none about the future. That was weird, when you thought about it, since people always spent their lives in the future, not in the past. Her chest tightened a little in excitement. What did it look like, this future?

In the doorway to the next room, she stopped dead.

It was *beautiful*. The walls shimmered with pale colors, always changing. The room looked as if each surface was a giant computer screen on the most delicate screen saver possible, and a screen saver that never repeated itself. The patterns it made did wonderful things to her mood, helping her feel cheerful and able to tackle anything. No, more than that—the patterns made her feel inspired in the same way poetry did. "Beauty is truth, truth beauty . . ."

"Cool walls," Jason said. But he didn't seem affected by their beauty the way Sharon was. She had almost decided he was a clod when he turned to her and said, "You really get off on them, don't you, Sharon? You got an artistic streak."

She only nodded, overwhelmed that he'd noticed her reaction. Maybe he wasn't a total clod after all.

The middle of the room held a huge table with fourteen chairs. Dr. Cee, Dr. Orgel, Jason, and Sharon sat down in four of them. Then another door opened and five more people came in. Two more doctors, three kids.

Sharon blinked. These kids weren't from 1999. No way.

"Welcome," Dr. Cee said. "I think I better make introductions. I'm Dr. Cee and this is Dr.

Orgel. This is Jason Ramsay from the United States, 1999. Sharon Myers, also from the United States, 1999, although from a different state.

"This is Jofrid Sigurdsdottir, from Iceland, 987."

From 987! So these people yanked kids from a thousand years further back in the past than 1999! Jofrid Sigurdsdottir was small, although her face looked older than Sharon's. She had reddish-blond hair in two very long braids, tied with green wool strips that matched her long green wool skirt and blouse. Around her waist was a wide embroidered sash with a leather pouch hanging from it. Sharon saw her spot Jason, who was at least a foot and a half taller than she and the color of dark chocolate, and Jofrid's eyes widened. But she said nothing.

With a graceful wave of her hand, Dr. Cee indicated another Yank. "This is Robbie, from London, England, 1810. Robbie, do you have another name?"

"Never did. Robbie does me." He grinned. He was short, too. Sharon had read that in the past, people were smaller. Worse nutrition. That seemed to fit Robbie, whose teeth were brown and cracked. One tooth on the left side was missing. He wore very old and very dirty pants, a loose shirt, and new-looking leather boots that seemed a bit too big for him. What Sharon noticed most was that he didn't look scared. Nor did Jason or Jofrid. "Grit," Dr. Orgel had said.

Well, then, what was *she* doing here? Because she seemed to be the only one who was scared.

Sharon was trying not to show it, but she was terrified.

Dr. Cee nodded toward the last boy, who was as different from Robbie as could possibly be. "This is Sor Spo Gillen, from right now, 2336."

"Hello," Sor said. He wore blue shorts and a plain white shirt with a strange little cape. Not quite as tall as Jason, he had dark brown hair, blue eyes, perfect teeth, and a well-muscled body. In fact, he was the handsomest boy Sharon had ever seen. All four doctors were handsome, too. Did the future build in beauty and health with genetic engineering? Or plastic surgery for everybody?

"And these are Doctors Riggin and Oa," Dr. Cee finished. "Now, I know you must all be bursting with questions. Ordinarily we'd take great pleasure in answering them, and in showing you Edge Station One. But just now—"

"Wait a sec, doc," Jason said. "What do you mean, 'ordinarily'? You folks yanked kids from the past before?"

"Oh, yes, several times," said Dr. Cee. "As you were told, only kids can t-port virtually anywhere ports exist. So we've needed to bring in teams before, for special missions."

The doctor ran her hand through her hair. Sharon saw that she was upset. These future people might need to use kid teams, but they didn't like doing it. They were concerned about kids' safety.

Usually nobody was concerned about Sharon's safety, except herself. Suddenly she felt better about this mission. Whatever it was.

"So where we going?" Jason said. "And to do what?"

Dr. Orgel spoke. He was still frowning. "I want to make one thing clear. Nobody *has* to go anywhere. The mission will be explained to you, and then you can each decline if you wish. Anyone who declines will be immediately returned to his or her own time."

"Everybody cool with that?" Jason said. He looked encouragingly at Sharon, Jofrid, Robbie, Sor. Only Robbie answered.

"Bang-up, guv'nor. Give us the lay of the thing."

"All right," Dr. Cee said. "The main point here is that we're very rushed for time. Ordinarily we'd take several days to train you, show you Edge Station, let you become a team. But this is an emergency!" Her voice rose and she bit her lip.

Another of the doctors took over. Sharon couldn't remember his name. He was older than the others, with white hair and twinkly eyes. He reminded her of a thin Santa Claus who worked out a lot.

"You need some background here, ladies and gentlemen. Sor, I'm going to repeat things you already know. Please forgive me. And the rest of you, please forgive my haste."

God, Sharon thought, these were the politest people she had ever met. They wouldn't last two minutes in a disagreement with her mother.

"Six years ago," the thin-Santa-Claus-doctor said, "the first alien race appeared at the edge of our solar system. Only a few of Earth's leaders ever got to see them. We call them the Gift Givers—or the 'GG's'—because they gave us the t-port booths and sally ports and some other technology that we'll show you after the mission. We don't know for sure why the Gift Givers came here, or why they gave us these things. But nothing has been the same on Earth since.

"The Gift Givers told us that they come from a distant galaxy. They say they have important business here in our galaxy. They're waiting for somebody . . . or something . . . and while they're waiting, they decided to help the *boon phylums*—"

"The what?" Jason said.

The Santa-look-alike smiled. "The boon phylums are a number of younger races, like humanity, who had been stuck in their own solar systems until the GG's helped them out. Just like us. The GG's told us we'd soon meet other alien races in our galaxy. And we *did*. Shortly afterward, some of those alien races started arriving in our own solar system through the sally-ports. From them we learned a little more about the Gift Givers. They—"

Suddenly da Vinci appeared in one of the empty chairs around the table. Just *appeared* there. Wasn't he supposed to be taking care of Tara? But, no, it wasn't da Vinci after all. It was a transparent three-dimensional image of da Vinci—what Dr. Cee had called a "PP." It was here to listen and communicate while da Vinci was someplace else.

Dr. Santa Claus didn't miss a beat because da Vinci's PP had materialized. "—help alien races to become super-races, with powers we only dreamed of before now. Powers—"

"Dreams are powerful omens," Jofrid said unexpectedly "A good dreamsayer can give advice of gold."

"Indeed." Dr. Cee smiled.

Jason said, "Powers? The Gift Givers promised to give humans powers? Like what? What are we talking here—flying faster than a speeding bullet? X-ray vision? Getting invisible?"

"No," Dr. Orgel said. "Better. Telepathy. Self-healing. The secrets of immortality. Interstellar travel. The ability to roam the stars."

"Good heavens!" Sharon said aloud, despite herself.

Jason said, "So what's the problem? Sounds good to me. These Gift Givers show up, hand out the goodies like Christmas morning, and—"

"No," Dr. Orgel said. "We have to *earn* the gifts."

"Well, okay," Jason said reasonably. "That's fair. No pain, no gain, right? So what do you got to do to get the goodies?"

"That's just it," Dr. Cee said. "We don't know. The Gift Givers won't tell us."

"They won't *tell* you?" Jason said. "An exam where the teacher won't tell you the questions?"

"Our best philosophers think that's part of the test. Da Vinci, give the background data. Short version, please."

The robot—or the transparent representative of the robot—spoke. It was weird to see the wall right through him while he answered.

"The Gift Givers are pretty vague, but we're reasonably sure that there are Nine Steps that a new race must achieve before it gets to move on to the next level."

"Next level?" Jason said.

"Races on that level get the supertechnologies I mentioned before. Plus, maybe they get the right to take part in whatever the Gift Givers are waiting for. Maybe."

It didn't seem to Jason that Dr. Orgel knew very much for sure. Still, Jason nodded. "Okay, when we get through all Nine Steps, it's like Graduation Day. So what are these Nine Steps?"

"The human race has fulfilled the First Step: We have colonized our own solar system. In other words, we graduated from our nursery— Earth—without blowing ourselves up.

"Our best philosophers think that the Second Step is demonstrating the initiative in advancement. In other words, the Second Step is going after the Third Step without waiting for it to be handed to us."

"No standing on the sidelines and whining," Jason said. "Yeah, good. Sounds like my basketball coach."

Sor said politely, "He sounds like a wonderful man."

Jason said playfully, "You brown-nosing, Sor?" Sharon knew it was the kind of thing guys said to each other when they were buddies, but Sor just looked confused.

Da Vinci continued. "Humans therefore have made every effort to find out for ourselves what the Third Step is. So far, we've failed. But then a complication occurred. The Gift Givers, you see, are also allowing other alien races to proceed through the Nine Steps. And while humanity would like to cooperate with the aliens, sharing whatever we discover, not all the alien races feel the same. In fact, two races in particular have turned out to be quite threatening."

"Here it comes," Jason said. "Competition time."

"Yes," da Vinci said. "These two races are the—Sharon, may I give the baby a chofflin?"

Sharon, startled, said, "A what?"

Dr. Orgel looked at Dr. Oa. "I told you there were still some bugs in the translation devices!"

Sor looked at Sharon and said kindly, "A chofflin is a sweet, sugar-based edible with no nutritional value but of considerable pleasure."

"Candy?"

"Data bank search, arcane languages . . . Yes. Candy. A 'lollipop.' "

"Sure," Sharon said.

"Thank you," da Vinci said. "Now, as I was saying, the two races who regard themselves as unfriendly rivals of humanity are the Devlin and the Panurish. The Panurish won't talk to us. Not even one word. But when a human ship moved close to a Panurish ship out beyond the solar system, they vaporized it. No warning, no discussion. They just vaporized it.

"And that was that."

5

"**V**aporized the ship?" Jason said, after a stunned silence. "Like, fried it? Killed everybody on board?"

"Yes."

Jason tried to imagine what it would be like to be vaporized in a single moment—to just no longer exist. Gone. Nada. Zilch.

Jofrid said quietly, "Very bad magic. The first law is hospitality. No stranger who comes to the homestead must be turned away."

"To the Icelandic in 987, yes," Dr. Cee said. "But obviously not to the Panurish now."

"Dangerous dudes," Jason said. "They the problem now?"

"Yes," da Vinci said. "But first a bit more background, please. When the Gift Givers first gave us sally ports and t-ports, it was a very confused time. For one thing, the Oort cloud of comets, which surrounds the solar system, was badly disturbed. Many comets fell on the cities of the United Solar System, causing widespread damage. Also, humanity didn't understand the new technology very well, and the Gift Givers don't explain. That's not their way. Some foolish things were done. For instance, humanity tried to send whole spaceships through to colonize new planets."

Jason said, "So what's wrong with that? A ship won't go through a sally port?"

Dr. Cee said somberly, "A ship will go through a sally port just fine. But adults cannot."

Sharon gasped. "You mean the ships went through the port to another planet but everybody died?"

"Everybody over about age sixteen," Dr. Cee said, which fit with what da Vinci had already told Jason. Something else didn't fit, though. Sor looked extremely upset at what Dr. Cee was saying, even though he must have known all this before. *Not good*, Jason thought. He didn't need an oversensitive wimp on his mission.

"The children of the colony ships probably survived," da Vinci said, "but of course none of them had been trained to operate ship equipment. They hadn't even finished their level eta studies. So we lost contact with those ships. We—"

"How many ships of kids are there out there someplace?" Jason interrupted. "Or—what did you call them? Lost colonies. How many shipfuls of kids on planets you can't contact?"

"Nine. But now we think we can reach one of them."

Jason suddenly stood up. "I'm feeling like I need to stretch before I take in any more. The rest of you feel like that?"

One by one, all the kids stood and stretched as Jason did. It did feel good, but what Jason really wanted was time to absorb all this stuff.

After all, three hundred fifty years had gone by! Even in school the history book chapters only asked you to take in a couple of decades at a time. Three hundred fifty years was a stretch.

"Okay," he said when they sat down again. "Let's wrap this up. Da Vinci, how are the Panurish connected to the lost colony? Give me the short form. You got seventy-five words, my man."

Da Vinci was silent for a minute. Then he spoke.

"Friendly aliens called Silb' anhurteara trade with us. They traded a communication cube that was shot into space by the captain of the colony ship to planet Jump just before the captain died. The Silb' anhurteara found the cube. The message said the information about Step Three was on Jump. But now we've learned that Panurish just t-ported to Jump. We need to get that second communication cube with the Step Three explanation before the Panurish do."

"Seventy-four words," Sor said. But Jason was less interested in the exact word count than in the stupendous meaning.

"You want to send us to Jump," Jason said. "To bring back this cube-thing with the Step Three play code on it, right?"

"Yes," Dr. Cee said. "If there were any other way, we wouldn't put you Yanks at risk. But there isn't any other way. And we *must* have that communication cube before the Panurish do!"

"Got it," Jason said. "But before we take off for Jump, can we listen to the other communication cube? From that ship captain who kicked the bucket?"

Dr. Cee hesitated. Dr. Oa said, "It's a little upsetting to watch. People dying in front of your eyes . . ."

Robbie said suddenly, "I seen three hangings. The last one was Black Jack Allen. Highwayman. His face turned purple and he bit off his tongue, lollin' out of his mouth like it was, black as bear's blood."

Sor turned pale. Robbie sat there grinning, casually scratching his head. Dr. Orgel said, "Bring the cube."

Da Vinci did, taking the cube, it seemed to Jason, right out of the solid wall. How did these people *do* that?

Da Vinci set the communications cube in the middle of the table. It was small, only about four inches on a side, and bright silver. How could anybody see any detail on such a small TV screen? Jason wondered.

He needn't have worried. The moment da Vinci said "Activate," a large transparent figure leapt out of the cube. Jofrid gasped and made a sign to ward off evil spirits. Robbie threw up one arm to shield his eyes and ducked under the table. But after a moment Jason saw it was only more light projections, like the PP's. No—more like some high-tech three-dimensional movie where you could view the action from all sides.

Robbie came out from under the table.

The projected figure was a man in some sort of uniform. His face was mottled with red marks and he spoke as if in great pain.

"Cycle six, day eight, year 2331. This is Captain Lej Cho Kenara of the United Solar System ship *Discovery* bound for the colony world Jump. I am dying. I send this cube into space back along our orbit in hopes it will go through the sally port. We landed a few minutes ago. All adults aboard have died or are dying. Only our children seem unaffected. Listen: *Adults cannot use sally ports.* But there is something else.

"A Gift Giver ship met us just beyond the sally port. A Gift Giver came aboard. He—she, it, I don't know—said they will land this ship on Jump so our kids will have a chance to live. But they will not stay, nor return the kids to Earth. They said that's . . . not . . . their way."

The man was growing visibly weaker. His eyes rolled back in his head. Jason had never seen anybody die, except on TV. But this was no actor. This was the real thing.

"No time," Captain Kenara gasped. It seemed to hurt him to talk, yet he kept on. "But Giver told . . . me . . . what the Third Step is. In order . . . to . . . 'right the balance for the young.' I recorded Step Three. Just . . . finished. Won't send with this . . . too dangerous . . . Please come to . . ."

He slumped to the floor.

Suddenly the perspective widened. Jason could see a huge room, with dead adults sprawled over chairs, on the floor. A small child tugged at a corpse and cried, "Mommy! Please, mommy!" Then the image disappeared and the small communications cube sat, silent and shiny, in the middle of the conference table at Edge Station.

Nobody spoke for a long time.

43

Finally da Vinci said, "That was over six years ago."

Jason said, "Okay, we got it. Our job is to find this second cube with Step Three on it before the Panurish find it and get powers before humanity, 'cause then they might fry us global. Let's go."

"Wait!" Dr. Cee said. "I know time is of the essence, but—"

"You bet your sweet point spread it is," Jason said. "Let's sally."

"—but we still need a formal decision from each of you on whether you accept this mission! We don't want to force anybody!"

"Fair enough," Jason said. "I'm revved to go. What about the rest of you—anybody want to bail? Sor?"

"I accept the mission," Sor said. He still looked pale from viewing the deaths aboard the *Discovery*.

"Jofrid?"

"It was foreseen that I would go on a long, dangerous quest. I dreamed it."

That must have been some dream, Jason thought. Aloud he said, "Sharon?"

"Yes. We—I'm going."

"Robbie?"

"Ain't nothing cow-hearted about Robbie, guv'nor."

"Da Vinci?"

Da Vinci said, "I am programmed to accompany this team." The robot sounded startled to be asked.

Jason stood up. "That's it, then. We're all in. Lead us to the sally port, Dr. Cee. Tip-off time."

Edge Station One wasn't on Earth.

"Come again?" Jason said. "We're *where*?"

"We're near Neptune's Orbit," Dr. Cee said.

"Like, Neptune the planet. We're already out in space," Jason said.

"That's correct. Now, don't get worried, Jason. Yanking you from Earth to Edge Station One was safe, and sending you from here to Jump will be safe, too. It's—"

"It's going to be *slow*," Jason said. "Isn't Jump, like, millions of miles away?"

"Seventy-three thousand, six hundred ninety light-years," da Vinci said helpfully. "Jump is on the far rim of the galaxy."

"Great," Jason said sarcastically, "so we make the world's slowest rim shot."

Dr. Cee smiled. "Yes, getting there would be slow if you were going by any means other than sally port. But the sally port, like t-porting, is instantaneous. Here, take your s-suit. The boys are changing in there."

"Oh." Jason couldn't think of anything else to say. Sally ports. Neptune. S-suits. What did the "s" stand for, anyway? How was he supposed to lead this mission when he had so little information?

He'd ask Sor. The twenty-fourth-century guy seemed a little wimpy—he'd been genuinely upset watching that tape of the dying Captain Kenara. No point in that—those people were already dead, and the thing to do now was get on with people still living. Still, Sor would be useful as a source of information. Coach Patterson always said that a good team captain utilized the strengths of his players. And, of course, da Vinci knew a lot of stuff, too.

Jason took his s-suit out of its package, stripped, and pulled the suit on. It fit perfectly. Made of some complicated woven material, it clung to his body from ankles to wrists to neck. Better hope Jump wasn't a hot place; he'd swelter. The package also contained boots and gloves. The gloves fastened onto a sort of hook at his waist. Jason looked at himself in a mirror: lookin' good. Sor, across the room, looked as natural in his suit as if he'd been wearing it all his life, which he probably had. He had an extra pouch of tools at his waist.

Then Jason saw Robbie.

The runt pulled his suit over a skinny body that nonetheless looked wiry and fast. Over the s-suit he put his baggy pants and loose filthy shirt from 1810. Jason saw that the inside of the shirt was sewn with at least a dozen pockets, some of which bulged with small objects. Robbie pulled on the s-suit's boots. Then he transferred from his own boots to the new boots a long, thin, wicked-looking knife.

Robbie caught Jason staring and said cheerfully, "Don't go nowhere without my tools, guv'nor. Not Robbie."

Jason said carefully, "Robbie, what exactly did you do in 1810?"

"Thief," Robbie said. "Pickpocket. Forking silver from gentry-morts. Whatever needs doing, guv'nor, Robbie's your boy."

Sor gasped, "You *stole* things? Things that didn't belong to you?"

"Belonged to me after I forked 'em," Robbie

said. "Nobody better. But don't you worry none, guv'nor. I'm keeping my fambles clean on this trip."

Jason felt that, as mission leader, it was his job to step in. "Does 'keeping your fambles clean' mean you won't steal anything while you're on my team? I hope so."

"You got it, guv'nor. Robbie don't steal nothing as long as he eats like they feed him here so far. Good food, and enough of it."

"You mean," Sor said scornfully, "that for you, ethical behavior persists only as long as everything goes well. You can't be counted on in a crisis."

"You calling Robbie cow-hearted?" His eyes narrowed. Jason saw him flex his fingers in the direction of his boot knife.

"Nobody's calling anybody names, not on my team," Jason said firmly. He moved casually closer to both boys; he was a foot and a half taller than Robbie, six inches taller than Sor. "That understood? Robbie?"

"Anything you want, guv'nor." Robbie looked sunny again, except for his eyes.

"Sor?"

"Certainly."

"Good man. Robbie, give me the knife."

Robbie didn't hesitate. He pulled it from his boot and gave it to Jason, who laid it on a shelf projecting from the wall.

"Robbie, you understand where we're going?"

"Out past Neptune and onto Jump."

"Yes," Jason said. "But you understand that they're different worlds? That already we're not anywhere on Earth?"

"Must be in heaven, then," Robbie said cheerfully.

Jason squinted at him. "No, we're . . . do you understand that we're going out where the stars are? Off the Earth completely?"

"Never are," Robbie said. "Can't be done, guv'nor. My advice is, just let the gentry-mort say whatever they like. You and me and Sor and the females, we just find this cube thing, and eat good while we're doing it."

So Robbie didn't even believe in space travel, Jason realized. In fact, Robbie probably didn't even understand that such things as other planets existed. Maybe Jofrid, who came from even further back in the past, didn't believe in outer space, either. What else didn't they know?

"Robbie, have you ever been to school?"

Robbie laughed. "Me? Never did, guv'nor. Learned on the street, Robbie did."

Sor said suddenly, "Why did you agree to go on this mission, Robbie? To eat regularly, yes. I've read the history of your time. But there is no reward for this mission, you know. Nothing you can bring back to your own time."

"Fine for all of me," Robbie said.

Jason said quickly, "Then let's go." They moved out of the changing room.

Jason was thinking furiously. Sor, from peaceful 2336, might be baffled by what Robbie stood to gain from the mission. But Jason knew better. There were a lot of guys in 1999 New York, some of them in Jason's own high school, who wouldn't mind disappearing to some new place for a few weeks. Either Robbie was hiding from someone who was after him in 1810, or else he didn't believe that he couldn't bring back loot from 2336 to his own time. Or both. Thief, outlaw, and what else? What kind of team was Jason supposed to lead on this mission?

Jason braced himself to see what had been going down with the girls.

But they both looked quiet. Jofrid wore her green dress over her s-suit. Well, if the future-types didn't object to that, Jason didn't. Sharon looked better in her suit than in her dorky 1999 dress, but she was carrying that damn baby, murmuring good-byes to it. Jason sighed. What a team.

"This way to the t-port chamber," da Vinci said, and they all followed.

The t-port chamber turned out to be a bare room with a booth in one corner. The booth had glass sides and looked a little like an old-fashioned telephone booth, the kind Superman used to change his costume in real old movies. Dr. Cee and Dr. Orgel waited nervously beside a desk covered with monitors, displays, keyboards, and strange-looking cubes.

To Jason's relief, the first thing Dr. Cee did was take the baby away from Sharon. "Are all of you ready?" Dr. Cee said. "Please remember, you can still change your mind."

"We're good to go," Jason said. No wonder these people needed help from kids from the past. They kept all the time talking about backing out instead of getting on with things.

"Then just a few more items of information," Dr. Orgel said. "The t-port on Jump was established by the Panurish, not by us, and in some ways it's not typical of t-ports. Da Vinci will explain how, after you arrive. The planet Jump is fairly Earthlike, but there are some differences. Both da Vinci and Sor have that data. Now, da Vinci will t-port first, to demonstrate what happens. Next, Sor, since he's t-ported before. Then—"

"Then me," Jason said. Didn't these doctors know that he was the leader? "Followed by the girls. Robbie, you defend the rear. Da Vinci, go."

The robot stepped into the booth. Dr. Orgel did something to the controls on his desk. For ten full seconds—Jason counted—nothing happened. Then da Vinci disappeared.

"He's already on Jump," Dr. Cee said.

Jason asked, "Can you get him back?"

"Only if he walks back through the port on that end. And this particular t-port is only open ten minutes a day—at sunset. Da Vinci will explain. Oh, I wish we had time to give you the usual training, but in this case, we just can't. Does anyone wish to back out?"

Give it a rest, lady, Jason thought. Sor walked to the booth, smiling and relaxed. He stepped inside, waited ten seconds, and vanished.

The booth was barely tall enough for Jason. He ducked his head a little and waited, suddenly nervous. Did these people really have the ability to send him to a distant planet where alien kids waited to fight him? Man, this was too weird, and if something went wrong . . . No, don't think like that. Stay focused.

Jason's last thought before he t-ported was, *I wish I'd double-checked that Robbie's knife really stayed behind.*

Jason vanished from the t-port booth.

He didn't see Jofrid's t-port, or Sharon's. Jofrid turned pale, set her lips together tightly, and left murmuring prayers. Sharon stood quietly, watching Dr. Orgel touch his controls. The second he finished, she darted out of the booth, grabbed Tara out of Dr. Cee's arms, and ran back. "Sharon!" Dr. Cee cried. Robbie sprang forward and tried to snatch the baby back. But it was too late. The ten seconds were up.

Sharon and Tara t-ported through the sally port to the planet Jump.

6

Sharon arrived on the first—and probably the *only*—alien planet of her entire life to the sound of screaming. From Jason. At her.

"That baby! You brought that damn baby! What's wrong with you, how could you—"

He sounded just like her mother! Sharon, shaken and scared, hadn't really meant to bring Tara with her. It was just that in the minutes before the t-port, she'd sort of lost it. Sharon had looked at Tara in a stranger's arms and had suddenly realized that she, Sharon, was going to go billions of miles away, leaving the defenseless baby with people Tara didn't even know. Sharon's mother had done that to *her* all the time when Sharon was little. She'd go to sleep in her mother's car and she'd wake up in some other car, or on some stranger's sofa, while her mother went out "partying" with new friends. Sharon would lie there too scared to cry, not knowing if the people would be mean or nice, not knowing when her mother would come back . . . or even *if* her mother would come back. It had been horrible. Looking at Tara in Dr. Cee's arms, all those scared feelings had come rushing back inside Sharon, and she'd acted without even really thinking. Nobody was going to make Tara feel that way. *Nobody*! So Sharon had dashed forward and snatched Tara and t-ported with her, and here was Jason yelling at her just the way her mother always screamed at her when Mom was drunk.

"How could you bring a baby on a dangerous mission like this, you stupid—"

Then Sharon really lost it. From fear, from old anger, from a sudden sick guilt that maybe she *had* endangered her precious little niece's life. She did something she'd never done before in her entire life: she screamed back at someone who was screaming at her.

"Don't yell at me! Don't you ever yell at me! You don't care what happens to Tara, you said you don't even like babies, you only care about what happens to your stupid mission because you're so stuck up about being the leader! Well, it's *my* mission too, and Tara is here so *I* can take care of her, and if you don't like it, Jason Ramsay, you can just stick it up your—up your—"

But she couldn't say it. She had never used language like that in her life before, and she couldn't use it now. It turned out she didn't need to. Jason was standing there looking stunned, as if she—quiet little Rose-of-Sharon Myers, who everybody told to speak up all the time— had hit him between the eyes with a two-by-four.

Jason said, "Well, uh, uh . . . well . . ."

Sharon felt someone put an arm around her. Jofrid. The Icelandic girl was really nice. And

Sharon found she needed the arm, because all of a sudden Tara was so heavy, and all of a sudden Sharon felt like she might cry.

Jason pulled himself together. His face smoothed out, and Sharon could see him make a huge effort to speak in a different voice.

"Well, uh, yeah. I'm sorry I yelled at you, Sharon. I shouldn't do that, I know. But I just see that baby here and I'm, like, hello? You know what I mean, don't you?"

And the weird thing was, that Sharon did know. She could see how Jason could lose it. After all, hadn't she, Sharon, just lost it herself? She'd actually *yelled* at this tall enormous boy! Her!

"But the thing is," Jason said reasonably, "Tara can't stay. It could be too dangerous for her here. She can just go back through the t-port gizmo, and since you got to take care of her, you go back, too. *Now*, before it closes for the day. Remember that Dr. Cee said it's only open at sunset, and she also said that all you got to do is turn around and go back through the port, right there? See?"

Sharon looked where Jason pointed. Rising up from the ground was a faint rectangular shimmer, like a ghostly door. Beside it stood Robbie, who must have t-ported in while Jason and Sharon screamed at each other.

And behind and around and under the shimmery t-port door was an actual alien planet.

Sharon caught her breath. She'd been so busy yelling and trembling that she hadn't even looked at Jump. She looked now.

It was early evening, and a yellow sun hung

low on the horizon, casting long shadows. That much was like home. But nothing else was.

The hilly ground was covered with a purple vine instead of with grass: a purple vine with millions of tiny little leaves, each no bigger than Sharon's thumbnail. It made the ground seem fuzzy, like the whole planet had purple fur. There were no big trees, but clumps of bushes dotted the hills, greenish-purple bushes with yellow flowers and clumps of shiny fruit. Somewhere a bird—or something!—sang a low, melodious almost-song. The air smelled fresh and tingling, sort of like lemons mixed with pine needles. And in the darkening sky hung one, two, three . . . six moons. Six.

It was the most beautiful and strange place Sharon had ever seen.

Jason was still talking in his reasonable, mission-leader voice. ". . . and so best for everybody if you just turn around with Tama and t-port back."

"Tara," Sharon said. "Her name is Tara."

"Whatever. You just do a one-eighty, Sharon, and hang with Dr. Cee and the other docs until we finish here and—"

"No," Sharon said quietly.

"No?"

"No. I'm staying. And so is Tara."

Jason kept on smiling, although his eyes darkened. "Now, Sharon, babe, that isn't a good idea. Not a good idea at all. A baby here—"

"Tara isn't in any danger. Look at this place! It's calm as . . . as . . ."

A piece of the Keats poem from English class came into her mind: *"Thou foster child of silence*

55

and slow time . . ." That was how she felt here, like Jump had adopted her, made her a foster child of this peaceful quiet alien countryside, away from her awful mother, away from everything that was wrong with her life in 1999. Jump felt *safe*, which might be weird, but it was true. Safe for her, safe for Tara.

Jason was waiting for her to finish her sentence. "As calm as what, Sharon?"

"As a 'foster child of silence and slow time.' "

"Come again?"

"Never mind. Tara and I are staying here. Both of us."

Then Jason lost it again. "No, you aren't! You think I want a baby on my team, crying and messing its pants and smelling awful and causing everybody all kinds of trouble—you're going back, girl! Now!"

"Let me go!" Sharon cried, because Jason had put one hand on her arm and started pushing her gently toward the shimmery t-port door.

And then everything happened at once.

Jofrid sprang forward like an angry tiger and started bawling out Jason. "Let her make up her own mind! Who do you think you are, the master of Allthing? A woman may choose for herself just as much as a man, no matter what the skalds sing us, and you remember that!"

Sor put a strong hand on Jason's arm. "We do not indulge in violence, Jason. Civilized people can settle differences without violence."

Robbie sidled up with a long, thin knife that had appeared from nowhere and said, "Let go the female, guv'nor, if you knows what's good for you."

For a long moment everybody froze, looking at Robbie. Sharon had never seen anybody's eyes look that scary. But then Robbie smiled, although he still held the knife. "Now, you know Robbie don't want to hurt nobody. You just let go of the young gentry-mort, guv'nor."

Jason let go of Sharon.

The tall black boy looked bleakly at Robbie, then Sharon, then Sor, and finally Jofrid. "Okay, folks. This is it. Look—the t-port's gone."

Everyone looked. The shimmery rectangular door had vanished. Sharon felt a thrill go down her spine. The sky was still full of fading light, but the sun had slipped below the horizon. While they argued and fought, the t-port had closed. It wouldn't be back until sunset tomorrow.

Jason said quietly, "You guys want a new leader?"

At that moment Sharon astonished herself. She heard herself saying firmly, "No. You're our leader, Jason. But Tara and I stay."

Robbie said, "That's good enough for Robbie."

Jofrid said, hanging her head, "Please forgive my boldness. It's not my place to challenge for leadership."

Sor said tightly, "The computers chose you, Jason. Their programs have been designed by the solar system's best minds. You should therefore remain in charge of this mission. But no violence." He stared in horror at Robbie's knife.

Sharon saw Jason draw a deep breath. He looked shaken. But his voice was steady when he said, "Okay. Tara and Sharon stay. But from

57

now on, *I* make the decisions for this group. Everybody cool with that?"

He looked hard at each face. Slowly everyone nodded. Jason held out his hand. "Robbie, give me that knife."

Robbie handed him the knife at once. He said cheerfully, "Anything you say, guv'nor."

"Then let's get going. Da Vinci . . . Sor, what's wrong with da Vinci?"

The robot stood by the sally port, slumping forward on its tin-can-like body, motionless. It looked dead. Sor made an annoyed clicking sound.

"It's this advanced model, Jason. Da Vinci's a UT6005. His smart programming is wonderful, but all the 6000-series 'bots have been unnerved by the coming of aliens to Earth. It wasn't in their initial programming, you see. Every so often something they perceive is so alien it makes a sort of loop in their circuits, and they just shut down everything else to contemplate it."

"Contemplate?" Jason said. "You mean, like, think about it?"

"Yes, basically."

"And da Vinci's just shut down for good? Gone?"

"Oh, no," Sor said. "I can jog him off the logic loop."

"Well, do it, then."

Sor stepped up to da Vinci and fiddled with something in the robot's neck. After a moment da Vinci straightened up and said, "Thank you."

Jason said. "He working again?"

"Yes."

"But he's just going to cut out and 'contemplate' like that any time something looks too new? And we don't know when he might do it?"

"I'm afraid so," Sor said.

"Great," Jason muttered. "Just what we need. A robot that goes spla."

"I am fully functional now," da Vinci said pleasantly, "and can advise you on any topic."

"Fine," Jason said. "Advise away. Dr. Cee said this t-port isn't typical. What did she mean?"

Da Vinci answered immediately. "T-ports exist all over the galaxy. They're like bus stops in your time—once you know where they are, you can travel wherever they go. Some t-ports are hubs, and from them you can go to many different places. Others only lead in one direction. This t-port is a terminal stop, because we're very far out on the galaxy rim. In fact, humans had no idea this t-port even existed until a few days ago, when the computer detected activity through it. Probably it was the Gift Givers; they're the only ones who know where all the t-ports are. If we had discovered this t-port six years ago, maybe a robot could have gone through it to get the kids from the *Discovery*. But we didn't know it existed. We only knew about the sally port, out beyond Jump's moons."

"Okay, so now Jump is on the bus map," Jason said. "What else?"

Da Vinci continued. "Most t-ports are open all the time. But we're in a section of the rim called the Torvil Anfract. Here, local space-time structure is contorted and folded and generally convoluted, resulting in unusual dislocations and multiple connectivities, further resulting in intermittent-only wormholing."

"Come again?" Jason said. "In English."

Sor said, "He means we're in a sector of space so strange that it takes too much power to keep a t-port open all the time. So this t-port is only open ten minutes each sunset."

"Why sunset?" Sharon said, interested despite herself. She shifted Tara to her other hip.

Sor smiled at her. "We don't know. Maybe the Gift Givers set it up that way so it would be easy to remember."

"Whatever," Jason said. "Now let's get going. Which way is the *Discovery*? It's getting dark."

Da Vinci said, "The *Discovery* is one-half mile in that direction."

The Yanks started walking. Immediately Sharon realized that it felt slightly weird. When she took a step, she seemed to go farther than she should. She felt light, and Tara felt lighter than usual in her arms. The others seemed to feel it, too—little Jofrid almost seemed to float along.

Sor grinned. "Great, isn't it? Jump is point eight eight Earth gravity. That means you weigh less here and can leap higher."

Jofrid said, "Powerful magic! What other magics be here?"

Da Vinci said. "Air composition is similar to Earth's. Jump has no axial tilt, so there are no seasons. Land-to-mass ratio is—"

"Later, da Vinci," Jason said. "Right now, everybody stay alert. The thing to do is get to the *Discovery* before dark."

The five Yanks and one robot walked up and down the gentle hills, Jason in the lead. Sor walked next. Sharon figured that Sor was second-in-command, the Yank with the tools and the answers, providing whatever the captain needed done. So what did that make her and Jofrid, walking together next, with Robbie and da Vinci somewhere behind them? But Sharon didn't mind; Jofrid was nice. Sharon shifted Tara in her arms to talk to the Icelandic girl.

"Thank you for sticking up for me, Jofrid, in front of Jason."

"I should not have done it."

Sharon felt hurt. "Why not? Do you think I'm wrong to keep Tara here?"

"No," Jofrid said. "A family must care for its own. It's a shame to leave kin in the care of strangers. But I should not challenge the men. I have been reprimanded at the Allthing for this unmaidenly fault."

Sharon struggled to understand. "You mean, where you come from, girls can't contradict boys? That's silly!"

Now Jofrid looked shocked. "It's the law."

"Not here, it isn't. Why, Jofrid, girls are just as—" But before Sharon could finish her sentence, two wild animals jumped out of a clump of bushes and dashed right toward the Yanks!

Tara screamed. The animals ran on all fours, hurtling dark purple shapes, with skinny bodies and big, earless heads. In those heads gleamed a mouthful of sharp white teeth between two gleaming white tusks. As they ran the animals made a shrill, grinding noise like car brakes just before a crash. Sharon had never seen anything so terrifying. They came straight at her and Tara, running and running and running . . . un-

61

til just before they were on top of her. Then they turned slightly aside and ran past, one on each side of her. She heard them crash into another clump of bushes, through it, and keep running.

"Keep calm, people, don't panic!" Jason was calling.

Sharon clutched Tara tighter. The baby was crying hysterically and trying to climb up Sharon's head. Sor looked pale, pointing some instrument in the direction the animals had run past. Jofrid was murmuring prayers, or spells, or something. And Robbie stood there with his knife in his hand.

"How'd you get that knife back *again*?" Jason roared.

"Forked it off your boot, guv'nor," Robbie said with his sunniest smile. "Just thought I could use it better'n you, if needs be. Maybe Robbie should keep the cleaver, then?"

"Oh, all right, keep it!" Jason said. He looked really harassed. "But if you pull it on a person again, I'll take you apart, you little runt, and don't you forget it!"

"Never will, guv'nor," Robbie said, still smiling "You can trust Robbie. Keeping my fambles clean."

Sharon doubted that, but she had her hands full trying to calm down Tara. While she patted the baby and walked her around, Sor said, "I have a reading on that creature, Jason. It's warm-blooded, with a three-chambered heart. Fairly primitive brain and nervous system. High heartbeat for its size, speed greater than expected, and mostly hollow bones. It's almost certainly carnivorous, with those teeth, but it will probably eat anything at all, to maintain that high metabolism. Sort of a cross between a bird and pig."

"Great," Jason said crossly. "*Pigbirds*. And what's wrong with da Vinci?"

"Contemplating again," Sor said. "I'll jog his circuits."

Sor fiddled with the robot. After a moment da Vinci said, "Thank you." Tara stopped crying and settled sleepily into Sharon's neck. Sharon heard Jason sigh.

"All right, Yanks, let's move it."

The five Yanks, one sleeping baby, and one robot set out again across the purple groundcover. The stars were brightening, silent shining lights of white, blue, faint red in the black sky. The fragrant lemon/pine-needle smell grew stronger. The six moons shone in the sky, and the hilly alien landscape looked just as beautiful as before. But Sharon shuddered.

Things weren't the same as before. *Almost certainly carnivorous, with those teeth,* Sor had said about the pigbirds. And he also said, *they probably eat anything at all.*

Sharon had screamed at Jason that Jump was safe for Tara. And now the t-port was closed, at least until sunset tomorrow. There was no way to take Tara back until then. Although once again, in the moonlight and brightening starlight, Jump certainly *looked* safe: a beautiful place of "silence and slow time." But what if it really wasn't? What if the pigbirds attacked, or the Panurish did, or something even worse the Yanks hadn't heard of yet?

What if Sharon had been completely wrong?

7

Jason, in the lead, was the first to see the *Discovery*. Despite himself, he stopped dead to stare for a moment. Not cool. A leader should take everything in stride, like he was prepared for anything. Well, tough on that. He, Jason, wasn't prepared for anything like the *Discovery*. No way. They didn't have stuff like this in Manhattan.

The ship was *huge*. As big as two city blocks, maybe three. Only one story, but still a monster. The outside was blackened and pitted. Jason couldn't see any doors.

"*Wellington* class," Sor said, beside him. "Intact. Captain Kenara said the Gift Givers landed her for the colonists, and it looks like they did a good job."

Jason said, "Why is it all black and scarred-up like that?"

"From entry into the atmosphere. Perfectly normal. But I'm surprised there aren't any open ramps. These big colony ships were designed to convert into buildings for the settlers to live in, with open courtyards and windows and everything. But this one is all locked up. Da Vinci, what do you think?"

"It's possible the ship *was* once converted to living space, and then reconverted to ship security."

"You mean," Jason said, "the kids left alive opened it up, lived in it awhile, then locked it tight all over again? Why would they do that?"

"I don't know yet," da Vinci said.

Robbie said, "Only good sense, guv'nor, keep everything under lock and key. Safer."

"From what?" Jason said, exasperated. "The colony kids are the only people on the whole planet!"

"Maybe it's protection against those animals. The pigbirds," Sharon said. Jason could tell she was afraid. He could see it in the way she stood, the way she clutched that dumb baby. Well, good. Let her be scared. It might keep her off his back.

Jofrid said, "Perhaps the house is locked for protection against trolls. Or against sleeping spirits."

"Yeah, right," Jason said. "Well, if so, we're gonna wake 'em up."

He strode to the *Discovery*. Up close, he could see the outline of a huge door, where the metal hull was supposed to fold down to make a ramp twenty feet across. Jason knocked on it hard.

"Hey, lost colony kids—let us in! We're human like you, and we just got here on the planet! We got your ride home! Let us in!"

Nothing happened.

"You are knocking on the cargo bay," da Vinci said. "It is possible that no one can hear you."

"Well, where should I knock?" Jason demanded. "I don't see any welcome mat and front doorbell!"

"It would be better to knock on the crew entrance, which is sensitized for general notification of the living quarters," da Vinci said.

"Fine," Jason said. "We'll knock on the crew entrance. Where is it?"

"This way," da Vinci said.

They all trudged the length of the great ship. Jason looked behind him at his team. Robbie, he noted, stuck close to da Vinci. Jason didn't think that the reason was fear; as far as Jason could see, Robbie wasn't afraid of anything. It must be that the runty nineteenth-century thief just liked the robot. Although what on earth did Robbie think that da Vinci *was*? But then Jason noticed something else.

"Sor, why are *you* carrying that baby?"

"I'm sure she gets very heavy for Sharon to carry all the time."

"Well, that's her problem! I might need you to fight, man, and there you are with a baby in your arms!"

"Fight what?" Sor said reasonably.

"How do I know? Pigbirds, maybe! Give Sharon the baby."

"All right."

The next time Jason looked back, Jofrid was carrying the baby, and scowling fiercely at Jason's back. She stopped it as soon as he caught her eye, lowering her head modestly. Jason wasn't fooled. That Jofrid might have to pretend to be demure and maidenly and all that crap in old Iceland, but she was nobody's doormat. And now she was mad at Jason for not liking Tara.

What a team.

They reached the crew entrance and Jason knocked as hard as he could. Nothing happened.

Next they walked around to the vehicle bay and knocked on that. Nothing happened.

Then they tried the passenger entrance. Nothing.

"We're almost back where we started," Jason said. "We've walked around the whole ship! Why won't they let us in?"

"Maybe no one is home," Jofrid said.

"Improbable," da Vinci said. "More likely they are barricaded inside."

"But why?"

"Just good sense," Robbie repeated, with some satisfaction. Jason could see that Robbie wasn't unhappy that Jason was wrong. "Keep locked up tight against thievery, guv'nor."

"Like yours, I suppose," Sor said coldly. He was carrying the baby again. This time Jason said nothing about that. He'd antagonized everyone enough already. Time to act like a leader.

"Okay, here's what we're going to do. It's almost dark. We're going to make camp over there, close enough to see if anybody comes out of the ship during the night. We're going to light a few fires, both so's the kids inside can see us and so's we can use torches against any pigbirds that bother us in the night. We're going to stand guard in shifts, two hours on each, all night."

"A good plan," Sor said, nodding. "Is that how life is arranged in your native Manhattan?"

Actually, Jason had seen the guarding-the-camp-all-night stuff in some movie. But no need to tell Sor that. Instead, Jason said, "Does anybody have anything to add?"

"What do we eat?" Robbie said.

"Good question. Sor?"

"In the morning I can test the fruit on those purple bushes for edibility," Sor said. "I have the right instrument to do that. Meanwhile, our packs have a limited amount of liquid nutrient. But the colony kids had better open up tomorrow, or we'll run out of food and have to t-port back tomorrow at sunset."

"We aren't t-porting back without that communication cube," Jason said firmly. "Unless you mean we just send somebody for a quick trip to pick up supplies."

"We can do that," Sor said.

"Good. What about water?"

Jofrid said, "This land has many springs, like Iceland. I noticed two as we walked here. If the water proves clear and clean, we could camp beside a spring."

"Okay, back to the spring," Jason said. "That's water solved. Now all we got to do is last twenty-four hours in the cold."

Sor smiled. "Not even that. You'll be surprised how warm your s-suit keeps you. And the liquid nutrient is laced with hormonal additives to quell appetite."

Jason wasn't sure what that meant, but he decided not to ask. No use looking even more uninformed than he already felt. Trying to look in command, he followed Jofrid to a sheltered place between two slight hills with a clear view of the *Discovery*. A small spring bubbled from a fuzzy purple hillside. Sor tested the water using a device in his pouch, and said, "Clean and drinkable. You each have an expandable cup in the sleeve of your s-suit." Sor was right; the water tasted wonderful.

Without being asked, Jofrid gathered sticks and handfuls of vines and started two small fires.

"Hey, thanks, Jofrid," Jason said, smiling at her. She didn't smile back. Still mad because he criticized the baby.

"You did that so fast," Sor said. "How did you know what would burn? And how did you start the fire?"

Jofrid did smile at Sor. "This land looks like my homestead, at Langerfoss. There I feed the fires for cooking, when the thralls are busy elsewhere. I lit the fire with this." From a pocket on her green dress she pulled what looked to Jason like two rocks.

"A flint fire-maker," Sor said. "Good."

The five Yanks sat with da Vinci around the fire, drinking liquid food from long flexible tubes that turned out to have been sewn into the backs of their s-suits. Jason hadn't even known they were there. The liquid food, whatever it was, tasted good. Even Tara sucked at it greedily. The night air felt cool and bracing on Jason's face, but everywhere else, his suit bathed him in warmth.

"Hey," Jason said suddenly. "What about Tara? She doesn't have an s-suit to keep her warm."

"I know," Sharon said.

Jason remembered how he'd first seen Tara:

tucked inside Sharon's bulky winter coat. "Can you stick that baby down inside your suit with you?"

"I tried. She won't fit."

Jofrid said, "I can give you my wool dress to wrap her in overnight. Only . . ." Her voice trailed off.

She doesn't want to wear a tight suit in front of guys, Jason thought. How did he know that? In the 1990s, babes turned up at the beach—even at school—in clothes that left nothing to anyone's imagination. But Jofrid, Jason sensed, was different. Girls from 900-whatever Iceland didn't go to sleep-overs without lots of body-hiding wool around themselves. Still, here was Jofrid offering anyway, so Tara wouldn't freeze.

The only other one with personal clothing on top of the s-suit was Robbie. Jason waited for him to offer his clothes to Tara. But he didn't. The runty street thief went on sucking his dinner from a tube, smacking his lips and ignoring Sharon and Jofrid.

What else besides a knife did Robbie have hidden in those loose inside pockets? If Jason asked, Robbie probably wouldn't tell him.

Sor said coldly, "Robbie, Sharon needs your clothing to keep Tara warm."

Robbie said cheerfully, "Can't do it, guv'nor. Robbie don't part with his togs for nobody."

Sharon said quickly, "That's all right. They're . . . never mind, it's all right."

"They're filthy anyway," Sor said. "You're right, Sharon. The baby would probably come down with bubonic plague."

"Bubonic plague was not active in London in

1810," da Vinci said helpfully. "Although it should be noted that Robbie's garments do indeed carry fleas. However—"

"Fleas!" Sor said, in total horror. He and Sharon instantly moved farther away from Robbie. Jofrid looked puzzled. All of a sudden, Jason realized that Jofrid might have fleas, too. In 900-whatever, weren't fleas common? Or not? Jason wished he'd paid more attention in history class.

Da Vinci was still talking. "—problem of keeping Tara warm is easily solved. I am able to generate heat along the length of every limb. Give me the baby."

"Well . . ." Sharon said.

"It's quite all right, Sharon," Sor smiled. "Da Vinci is absolutely reliable about his own programming."

Sharon handed Tara, who was nodding sleepily, to the robot. It laid her on a cushion of vines, then lowered its tin-can body to the ground beside her. With its tentacles it made a circle completely around Tara. Sharon put her hand inside the circle.

"Why, your arms are just like electric heaters, da Vinci! It's like Tara's lying in a heated bed!"

Jason had a sudden unpleasant thought. When the pigbirds had gone howling by, da Vinci had gone into "contemplation" mode, shutting down. What if some new alien animal showed up during the night and da Vinci shut down again? Would Tara freeze?

Jason decided not to mention this. Probably if Tara got cold enough, she'd wake up and start yelling. Anyway, it was Sharon's problem.

But there *was* a problem that was his. He sat up on guard shift, thinking about it. There was nothing to see anywhere around him except darkness, smelling a little like lemons, and the low flames of the two small fires, so he had a lot of time to think.

He was supposed to be the leader of this mission. But they'd only been on Jump a few hours, and already Jason had everybody on his team mad at him, except da Vinci. Sharon and Jofrid were upset because Jason didn't like Tara. Robbie was out of control—he'd never been *in* control. He'd use knives or anything else he felt like, no matter what Jason said, and smile sunnily while he did it. Sor was polite to Jason—that guy would be polite on the *Titanic* while it sank under him—but Jason had also seen the doubt in Sor's eyes. Sor wasn't sure Jason could lead this mission. All Jason had done so far was yell at the girls, make Tara cry, and give Robbie orders that Robbie didn't follow.

Things were going to have to change, Jason realized. He was going to have to turn it around. By himself. Think more before he spoke.

Accept that Tara was here, at least until the t-port opened tomorrow night.

Remember that these kids weren't like the buds and babes at Benjamin Franklin High. They were whole different stories. Jofrid believed in trolls and evil spirits. Robbie was used to stealing whatever he needed, and fighting to keep it. Sharon had some kind of weird super-responsibility thing for that baby. And Sor turned pale at the first sign of anybody dissing anybody, even at stuff that in Manhattan would just be buds hanging together and joshing.

He sighed. This mission was going to be more complicated than he thought. And that was before they even got inside the *Discovery* to look for the communications cube!

Still, it was his mission. His, Jason William Ramsay. And he was going to do it, and keep his team together in the meantime. Stay focused. Make it work.

He even had some ideas how he might do that.

8

When Sharon awoke in the morning, everybody else was already up. Instantly she groped by her side for Tara. Then she saw that the baby sat on the ground a few feet away, sucking on a tube of nutrients left over from the night before. Bits of leaves clung to Tara's hair and overalls, but she smiled happily and waved her chubby fists in the air.

"Hey, Sharon. Morning," Jason said. "How you doin' today?"

Sharon looked at him. He looked a lot friendlier than he had the night before. Maybe something good had happened. She said, "Good morning. Did the colony kids open up the *Discovery* for us?"

"Not yet," Jason said. "But they will today. You need anything for Tara?"

Sharon just stared. Jofrid, sitting on a rock nearby, rolled her eyes. Sharon managed, "No, thanks."

"Then you get yourself put together soon as you can. We're going to crack that starship!" Jason went off whistling.

Sharon whispered to Jofrid, "Why is he in such a good mood?"

"I don't know. He praised me much for my rope."

"Rope? You know how to make rope?"

Shyly, Jofrid showed her. Jofrid had cut some of the vines that grew all over the ground and stripped off all the tiny purple leaves. The stems were long, flexible, and very tough. Jofrid had braided them together for even greater strength.

"Great," Sharon said. "What will you do with the rope?"

"Set snares for a pigbird. Robbie can kill it with his knife, and we can roast it."

Sharon was horrified. "Eat one of those awful *pigbirds*? Ugh! And Jofrid—you don't even know if it's poisonous. Besides, Sor is going to go back through the t-port tonight and bring back supplies."

"What we wish does not always come to pass," Jofrid said. "It's best to be prepared for the worst. And Sor can test the pigbird meat in his device. He already tested the purple fruit. We can eat them. Have one."

She held out a fruit to Jofrid. It was the color of a plum but the size of an apple, with a smooth shiny skin. Sharon said, "No, thanks. I better see to Tara."

"I changed her wrappings," Jofrid said. "I hope you don't mind. Jason said to let all sleep who could do so."

Sharon went over to Tara. How could Jofrid have "changed her wrappings"? Sharon had no extra diapers with her, a fact which had already worried her. She opened Tara's snowsuit and investigated.

Jofrid had removed the baby's dirty diaper, washed her, and put back on a new diaper made of Tara's thin tee-shirt filled with a soft moss that, Sharon could see, would absorb moisture just fine. "What a good idea!"

"It is how we do at Langerfoss," Jofrid said. Her eyes glowed at Sharon's praise.

Why, she likes me! Sharon thought, wonderingly. She wants to be friends!

The two girls smiled at each other. Sharon said, "Would you show me how to make rope from vines? And to start fires, the way you did last night?"

"Yes," Jofrid said happily. "Will you teach me the sagas of your homestead?"

"What are sagas?"

"Stories and poems. I would like to be a skald one day, even though the Allthing says no woman must do so."

"Sure, I'll teach you poems and stories," Sharon said. "I love English class. What's a skald?"

"A sayer of sagas and ballads," Jofrid said.

"Pooh, girls can do that," said Sharon. "Hey, why is Jason waving at us like that?"

Jofrid looked. "I think he wants us to go with him and Sor. Where's Robbie?"

"I don't know. But we better go with Jason. Maybe the colony kids have opened up the *Discovery* to let us in."

That, however, did not happen.

The five Yanks and da Vinci approached the

Discovery the same way they had the night before, circling the whole ship and knocking on every door or bay. Nothing opened up. When they were back where they'd started, da Vinci said, "They don't respond."

"No kidding," Jason said. "The next move is up to us. Can they see us out here, even without opening any windows?"

"Oh, yes," da Vinci said. "The *Discovery* is equipped with 360-degree viewscreens."

"Great," Jason said. "Then we're gonna give them something to look at."

"What?" Sor said.

"First, the whole story of why we're here. The t-porting, the communication cube, the Third Step for humankind, the Panurish . . . all of it. Da Vinci's gonna do that."

"I am?" da Vinci said.

"You sure are," Jason answered. "You tell information real good. So you stand here and say the whole story over and over, da Vinci."

"As you wish," the robot said.

Sor said, "And what are we going to do?"

Jason said, "We're going to play football."

The others looked at him as if he'd gone nuts. *Football?* Sharon thought. What good would *that* do?

Sor said, "What's football?"

"See, that's the thing," Jason said. "You don't know football in 2336. The kids inside the *Discovery* don't know it. But when they see us all running and hollering and having a great time playing, they'll be curious. They'll *want* to know about it. So they'll come out to ask."

Sharon doubted that. But maybe she was

wrong, maybe at least the boys inside the *Discovery* would want to know about football. Maybe it was a guy thing. But how were they going to play with only three guys?

"Me and Robbie will be one team," Jason said, "and Sor and Sharon and Jofrid will be the other."

"Me?" Sharon said. "I don't know how to play football!"

Jason smiled at her, the same smile he'd given her at the campfire. He was certainly being nicer this morning. "That's good, Sharon," Jason said. "It's good you don't know, because neither does Sor or Robbie or Jofrid, so we'll all be sort of even. Me, too, because even though I know what the football rules are, my high school doesn't have a football team. I played basketball."

Sor said, "Then why don't you teach us basketball instead?"

Sharon said, "We are *not* even. Look how much bigger you are, Jason. What if somebody gets hurt?"

Robbie said, "Robbie's not much for games, guv'nor."

Jofrid said, "Perhaps instead we should try to snare an animal to eat?"

Jason went on smiling, but his smile looked a bit strained, and he ran a hand over his hair like he didn't know he was doing it. Sharon felt a little sorry for him. He was trying so hard to be a leader.

Carefully Jason said, "We're not going to play basketball because we got no hoop, and nothing to fasten a hoop onto. It's true I'm the biggest one here but the teams are sort of even because mine only has two players and you got three. Nobody's gonna get hurt because we're going to play touch, not tackle. We don't need to trap an animal to eat because the colony kids are going to open up soon. And Robbie, you're going to be fine as a player. Good. *Great*. You're fast and you dodge well."

Sor said, "Is a ball required?"

"Yes. Right here."

Jason had made the ball, Sharon saw. It consisted of a wad of leaves wrapped around and around with cords of Jofrid's tough rope.

"Jason," she said, "is that ball going to stay stuck together if anybody kicks it?"

"Sure it is," Jason said. "Now, here's the deal. This is center field. The end zone on one side is between those two bushes over there . . ."

It took a long time, but eventually everybody understood the rules. At least, Sharon thought they did. It was hard to tell until they actually played. Sharon didn't really want to, but she didn't want to be a wet blanket, either. And maybe the game would convince the kids inside the *Discovery* that the Yanks were harmless. Who knew?

"Okay," Jason said. "Da Vinci, you stand here on the fifty-yard line and start telling our story. Sor, your team has the ball. Your goalposts are that way, remember. GO!"

Everything happened at once.

Sor bent over the ball and threw it backward to Jofrid, who caught it. She started to run forward. Instantly Robbie darted forward, grabbed the ball from her—how fast he was!—and started to run with it in the opposite direction. Sor jumped toward him, but Jason blocked his way. That left Sharon, who ran toward Robbie— wasn't that what she was supposed to do? But by the time she intercepted him, his hands were empty.

She hadn't seen Robbie throw the ball! Where was it? Wildly Sharon looked around, still running, and crashed into da Vinci, who was chanting, ". . . communication cube vital to Earth. If the Panurish get it—" The robot fell over, still chanting. Jason was screaming "Foul! Foul!" and Jofrid seemed to be tangled up on the ground in her own long green dress.

Tara, watching from the sidelines, clapped her little hands and laughed.

"Where's the *ball*?" Jason cried. "Who's got the *ball*?"

Nobody had the ball.

Jason stood in the "football field," scratching his head and looking bewildered. Jofrid untangled her skirts and staggered upright. Sor searched for the ball, but couldn't find it. Neither could Sharon. But she suddenly had an idea.

"Robbie, did you steal the ball and hide it?"

Robbie looked innocent.

"You did, didn't you?" Sharon said. "You flattened the ball and hid it somewhere under the vine groundcover!"

Robbie grinned. "The idea be that the other coves ain't to have that ball, right enough, miss? Well, they ain't having it!"

"No, no!" Jason cried. "That's against the

rules, Robbie! You can't remove the ball from play without penalty!"

"Nobody makes Robbie pay nothing, guv'nor," Robbie said. "I'll take anybody apart who tries, I will."

Suddenly Sharon got the giggles. The short nineteenth-century thief stood smiling at Jason, refusing to give back the "football" made of leaves and vines. And Jason looked as serious as if this were a game between two high schools that had been sports rivals for a million years. It was just too silly. But she tried to hide her laughter, because it seemed so important to Jason.

"Robbie," she said, "give Jason the ball."

"Never will, miss."

Jason cried, "But I'm on your team! We're on the same side!"

"Oh. Well, then," Robbie said. Reluctantly he walked to a place in the dense groundcover that looked to Sharon like every other patch of groundcover, and pulled out the football, slightly flattened. "Here it be."

"Fine," Jason said. "Ten-yard penalty to our side. Okay, second play. Jofrid, you stand here. Sor, Sharon—"

"—before the Panurish find the cube," da Vinci said earnestly to the closed starship. He, too, had pulled himself upright again. "So we came from Earth through the sally port—"

"Zero-zero, first down," Jason called, slightly desperately. "Play!"

On the second play, Sor captured the ball and started running. Sharon watched him admiringly. He ran so straight and strong and swift . . . until he suddenly pitched forward and fell onto his face in a patch of purple-leafed vines.

"Sor!" she called, running toward him. "Are you all right?"

"Yes, the leaves are soft," Sor said. "But something tripped me . . . a rope!"

"I made the snare and set it," Jofrid cried. She danced over the field in glee. "And it worked, it worked, it brought you down much better than Jason's 'blocking'!"

"Jofrid!" Jason roared, "Sor is on *your* team! You don't want to bring him down! He's on your team! And snares are illegal in football!"

"Oh," Jofrid said in a small voice. She stopped dancing around.

"—and so the Panurish have come to get the cube themselves," da Vinci said, "and we—"

"And where in blue blazes," Jason roared, "is the *ball*?"

Robbie grinned. He'd done it again, Sharon thought. He'd used his amazing powers of thievery to steal the ball right out from under their noses. This time Sharon couldn't hold in her giggles. She collapsed on the grass, laughing and whooping, while Jason tried to explain all over again that the game had rules, *rules*, and Jofrid tried to persuade Robbie to give up the ball, and da Vinci chanted on about communication cubes and the Panurish.

But the *Discovery* didn't open up. The football game might be the funniest thing Sharon had ever seen, but apparently the kids inside the starship didn't think so. Or maybe they didn't have a sense of humor. Whatever the reason, the starship stayed locked up tight, and the Yanks stayed on the outside.

By late afternoon, everyone was starved.

"Okay, team, we head back to the t-port now," Jason said. "Got to be sure to get there by dark."

Sharon found she was glad to go. Tara had taken a long nap but woken up cranky. The baby was hungry. Sharon was, too. It seemed a long time since they'd finished off the tubes of nutrients for breakfast. Her stomach growled as she trudged along with the others toward the t-port a half mile away.

"Everybody clear on the plan?" Jason said. "Sor, you and Robbie t-port back to Earth, grab as much food as you can carry, and find out what ideas Dr. Cee has for getting us inside the *Discovery*. Jofrid, you make us another fire. And Sharon, you take Tara back for good, right? You see now that this is no place for a baby?"

"Yes," Sharon said.

"You mean it, now? No last-minute switches like last time?"

"No," Sharon said. "I mean it."

And she did mean it. It had been a mistake to bring Tara to Jump. Sharon saw that now. She'd done it in blind panic, in concern for the baby. But the truth was, da Vinci could take care of Tara with a lot less strain than Sharon could. He'd done it all afternoon. And if da Vinci could care for Tara, then so could another nanny robot in 2336. Sharon loved Tara, but toting her around, changing her, amusing her twenty-four hours a day was harder than Sharon had expected. Babies were a lot of work. How come

Mrs. Northrup liked taking care of five or six of them in day care? Well, Mrs. Northrup was an adult. Maybe when Sharon was, too, she'd be happy to run a day-care center. But for now, she'd be glad to just go back through the t-port and turn the baby over to Dr. Cee.

Jason smiled at her. "Good."

They walked over the last low hill while the sun was still well above the horizon. The t-port place was marked by a bare patch in the ground-cover. The Yanks sat down around it, silent, and waited for the shimmer that meant a ten-minute door was open across billions of miles of empty space. A shimmery door to Earth.

Slowly the sun sank. Three of Jump's moons appeared in the sky, two in the east and one on the western horizon. One by one, the alien stars came out, silver and cold.

Twilight came and went. It turned full dark. And the door, which was supposed to be automatic, never shimmered and opened.

The t-port wasn't there anymore.

9

"**O**kay," Jason said. "Nobody panic!"

Actually, nobody looked panicked, but Jason felt that way. The other Yanks just stared, stunned, at the place the t-port should be.

"Da Vinci, you got any ideas why the t-port isn't here?" Jason said.

"No," the robot answered. "It should appear on time."

"Well, so should subways, and they're sometimes late," Jason said. He hoped he sounded reasonable. "We'll just wait a while. Meantimes, Jofrid, you work on that fire, okay? Sor, you and Robbie look around a bit, on the other sides of those hills, maybe the t-port just missed the spot a little."

"No," da Vinci said again. "Micropositioning is very accurate."

"Well, we can look anyway, can't we?" Jason said irritably. "Better than doing nothing."

He walked around the t-port site, squinting at it, hoping it would suddenly appear. Sor and Robbie disappeared over low ridges. Sharon bent over Jofrid's fire, feeding it bits of leaves. Tara started fussing again. Why couldn't babies have an "Off" switch, like computers? Tara would be better running as a background program.

Jason poked at the place the t-port should be. Nothing. All he felt was night air, getting colder. Unlike last night, the sky was cloudy, the stars and moons mostly buried under a hazy mist. Jason's s-suit switched itself on.

An hour later, the t-port still hadn't appeared. Sor and Robbie came back with armloads of the purple fruit that Sor's tester machine had said was all right to eat. It tasted good, but it wasn't very filling. The Yanks sat around the fire feeling hungry. No one said much. Too depressed, Jason thought. And it was his job to solve this mess. How was he going to get the Yanks something to eat? How were they going to get back to Earth? What if the *Discovery* kids weren't opening up the ship because they were all dead inside?

"Da Vinci," Jason finally said, "tell me everything you know about t-ports. Maybe there's something we missed, something we can check out here. Tell me everything."

Da Vinci said, "Everything? That would take seventeen point six three hours and—"

He was cut off by sudden terrible shrieking like demons out of the night. "EEEEIIIIIIIIIIII! EEEIIII! EEOOOOO-OOO-OOOO!"

Tara screamed. Everyone jumped up, looking around in terror. But then Jofrid smiled. "I caught one!"

One *what*? Whatever it was, Jason wasn't sure he wanted it caught anywhere near him. The shrieking went on and on. Sor turned on the laserlight in his tool pouch; it cast a powerful wide beam into the darkness. Jofrid and Robbie ran along the path of light, and after a minute the others followed.

Over the next hill, its foot caught in a snare, was a pigbird. And a second pigbird attacked it. The two darted at each other, shrieking and biting, flapping their wings. The noise was unbelievable, and so was the violence with which the two animals fought.

Robbie's eyes gleamed. "It's a cockfight!"

"A what?" Jason demanded.

"A cockfight, guv'nor. Ain't you never seen one? The sporting coves arranges them. To bet on. I'll give you a quid against quid-and-a-half on the one in the net. To the death."

Sor said, "You . . . you are . . ." Then he turned away and threw up in the bushes.

Jason felt a little sick himself. Nothing he couldn't handle. Boy, Sor was a wimp. He was gonna feel really ashamed when he stopped puking. Jofrid, Jason noticed, didn't seem upset at all. Probably there was lots of animal killing in Iceland in 984. Sharon had gone back to the fire, taking the screaming baby, which was good.

It was over in two more minutes. Robbie had been right; the pigbird trapped in Jofrid's snare had won, despite the vine wrapped around one of its feet. It looked wounded, flapping its wings feebly on the ground, but the other pigbird was dead.

As Jason watched in astonishment, Robbie stepped forward, grasped the snared bird around its neck, and killed it with his knife. And then Jofrid calmly stepped forward, picked up the other dead pigbird, and started pulling off its feathers.

"More meat on here than I thought," she said. "It will roast well."

Jason decided that he, too, should go back to the fire.

Sor was already there. To his surprise, Sor didn't seem at all ashamed of puking. "That Robbie is a barbarian even for his own time," he said. "He does not know how to behave in any circumstance."

"What do you mean?" Jason said.

"To bet on death . . . or on any kind of violence—it's weak and stupid."

"Weak? And it's not weak to, like, toss your cookies looking at a dogfight?"

"They're not dogs."

"Whatever," Jason said.

"No, of course it's not weak to have a civilized reaction to uncivilized behavior," Sor said, and now it was Sor who sounded astonished. "Do you mean you approve of Robbie's obvious relish for violence?"

Did he? Jason wasn't sure. He tried to sort it out. "Well, I didn't find it exciting like he did, no. And I wouldn't go betting on any fight to the death between any animals. But violence isn't always bad, Sor. Sometimes you got to defend yourself. And about killing animals—well, people got to eat."

"Violence is not justified except in extreme cases of self-defense, and then only with sorrow for the life you take," Sor said. "And eating meat is barbaric."

Jason didn't answer. No point in another argument. But Sor's distaste for violence made something suddenly clear to him. He said, "So that's why your Dr. Cee had to yank us from the past. I didn't really get it before. You guys in 2336 are too squeamish to do what has to be done."

"That's not true," Sor said angrily. "But betting on poor animals fighting to the death isn't necessary."

Jason couldn't argue with that. But he realized he had some doubts about Sor now. He was smart and cooperative, but was he too wimpy to be of use if the mission on Jump got rough?

There was no way to know. But at least Jason had learned one thing: He had two team members who were anything but wimpy. Robbie and Jofrid took killing as just part of the day's work.

Maybe that wasn't so good either.

Confused, Jason decided not to think about it. Instead he prowled around the camp, looking for the t-port. He didn't find it.

Jofrid and Robbie came back with the pigbirds, which had been defeathered and gutted, and were now headless. Reluctantly, Sor tested the meat in his safety device and pronounced it safe to eat. Jofrid rigged up a sort of grill out of green twigs over the fire and roasted the pigbirds, turning them often. In a short while they smelled delicious.

"When can we eat, Jofrid?" Jason asked. His stomach was growling hard.

"Soon," Jofrid said. She and Sor were roasting something else over the fire, some bumpy vegetable-looking things.

"We're calling these 'potatoes,' " Sor said. "I tested them for edibility; they're safe for us to eat."

Jason was struck by a question. "Hey, how come so much of this stuff is safe for us to eat, huh? I mean, humans don't come from Jump, right? We evolved on Earth. So how come we can eat Jump food? Da Vinci?"

Sharon said, "Da Vinci went into contemplation again when he saw the pigbird fight."

"Again? Well, Sor, start him up," Jason said. Sor did, and Jason repeated his question.

"Answer unknown," da Vinci said. He was rocking Tara on his mechanical shoulder. "But the best probability is that there are only so many ways life can evolve. On basically Earth-type worlds, life evolves with basically Earth-type chemistry. Although there is much vegetation on Jump that would be poisonous to humans. As there is on Earth."

"Great," Jason said, looking at the roasting vegetables. "But you tested these, right?"

"Of course," Sor said.

And when Jason tasted the "potatoes," they were good. So was the roasted pigbird, for which Jofrid had made a sort of sauce from the purple fruit.

"Man, we're all sure glad you're along, Jofrid," Jason said, when he finished eating. "You can do 'bout everything, girl!"

Jofrid flushed with pleasure. Sharon looked proud of her friend. Even Sor, who'd eaten no meat but had filled up on potatoes and fruit, had stopped glaring at Robbie. Robbie sat close to da Vinci, almost leaning against the robot. Everybody looked full, and warm, and sleepy.

Weird, Jason thought. Here they were maybe marooned on Jump, with nothing going right, and people looked *pleased.* It wouldn't last, of course—everybody knew that, too. They were all in deep doodoo, and this well-fed moment was just that: a moment. Tomorrow, Panic City.

But they might as well enjoy the moment while it lasted.

It lasted four more hours.

Sharon poked Jason awake. He'd been dreaming about the perfect basketball shot, a dunk so high and handsome that Kareem or Larry could have made it, only he, Jason, was the one who did. Then he felt Sharon's fist in his ribs and he jolted awake.

"Robbie's gone," Sharon whispered.

"Come again?"

"He's *gone,*" she hissed. "I just finished my guard shift and I was checking everybody before I woke Jofrid for her turn. And Robbie's not here. He must have sneaked away without me even knowing it!"

"Yeah, he's good at that." Jason sat up and looked around. The sky was much brighter than when he'd gone to sleep. The cloud cover had cleared, and there were five moons up, one full and low and very bright.

"What should we do?" Sharon said.

"Nothing," Jason answered. "No point in looking for him. If he doesn't want to be found, he won't be. And besides, seems to me he's pretty good at taking care of himself."

"Well, yes," Sharon said, "but—" She didn't

get to finish her sentence. Screaming started coming through the night. Not pigbird screaming this time—human screaming.

"From that way!" Jason said. "By the other spring!" He was on his feet in a minute, running toward the spring. In the bright star-and-moonlight he didn't stumble. After a minute he heard the others running after him.

At the spring he stopped dead. Robbie stood with his back to the hill, and his left arm choking the neck of a little girl who couldn't be more than seven or eight years old. Facing him were three other kids, two boys about ten and a beautiful girl who looked at least eighteen. In his right hand Robbie held his knife, still bloody from the pigbird.

"—don't want to hurt nobody, miss," Robbie was saying in a reasonable voice. "And I won't, neither. Alls I want is for you to listen—"

"Robbie!" Jason cried. "Let that little girl go!"

"Certainly, guv'nor. Soon as the gentry-mort here says she'll listen to me. Or to you."

"Of course we'll listen!" the older girl cried. "We'll do whatever you say! Just don't hurt Betta!"

"Nobody's going to hurt anyone," Jason said. Suddenly he felt calm, in control. It felt wonderful. He walked over to Robbie and took the trembling little girl from him, holding her firmly by the hand. Then Jason smiled at the older girl.

"Hi, how you doin'? I'm Jason Ramsay, from Earth, and this is Robbie—don't mind him, he just gets carried away sometimes. And you're from the *Discovery*, right? We been trying to get you to come out to talk to us for a whole day now. Did you know we were here? From Earth?"

"Earth? No! How . . . give me Betta first!"

Jason considered. Even if the four kids ran, he could easily overtake them and get at least the littlest one back. He let go of Betta's hand, and she ran over to the boys who, Jason now saw, were twins. All four kids wore what looked like different versions of s-suits.

"We're sorry Betta got scared," Jason said, smiling at the older girl. "We're on your side, gang. We just got here day before yesterday from Earth, and we been—"

"From Earth!" the girl cried. "You've come to rescue us!"

"Well, no . . . I mean, yes. We can take you back through the t-port, no wait, the t-port isn't there . . . Listen, I better tell you the whole story from the beginning. It's kind of complicated."

Sor stepped forward. "You are the only survivors of Expedition Delta, 2331, is that correct? Are you Annit Janna Wethel?"

"Yes!" the girl cried. "You *have* come to rescue us! We thought we were here forever!"

Maybe you are, Jason thought, *if we don't get the t-port back. And we might be here forever, too.* But it didn't seem a good idea to say this aloud. Instead he said, "Let's go inside, okay? Then we can explain everything."

But Annit was eyeing Robbie nervously. "He, too?"

"Yes," Jason said firmly. "He's a member of my mission. But he'll behave, I give you my word. Won't you, Robbie? You won't go upsetting anybody else?"

"Never would, guv'nor," Robbie said, with his broadest smile. Jason didn't believe him for a minute. Still, Robbie had been the only one to realize that the *Discovery* kids would probably come out for water eventually. Although, come to think of it, why had they come out for water? Didn't they have water-making stuff inside that wonderful future starship?

All at once Jason got a cold feeling in his stomach.

He said, "Uh, Annit, let me ask you something real quick. Have there been any aliens called Panurish around here recently?"

Annit cried, "How did you know? That's the reason the ship was on maximum security. They attacked four days ago."

Sor said quickly, "Were any of you injured?"

"No. They ignored us entirely. But the attack is why we had to get water from outside. They took everything!"

"Everything?" Jason said. "Like what?"

"Everything even a little technological," one of the twin ten-year-old boys said. "They even took furniture!"

"Looking for the communication cube," Sor said. "Furniture is programmable. They don't know what human communication cubes look like, so they took everything that might contain Captain Kenara's message about the Third Step."

"The what?" Annit said.

"Let's go inside," Jason said. "We got a lot of explaining to do."

*   *   *

The inside of the ship looked like a store that had just held the biggest going-out-of-business sale of all time. The place was huge, and it was *empty*. Holes in the walls, floors, and ceilings showed where things had been ripped out. All that was left was a bunch of blankets, a few pieces of simple furniture, dishes and glasses and cups and some simple toys for kids, and a lot of decorative objects—what Jason's mother called "knick-knacks"—for the vanished adults. No machines left except the lights, which seemed to be the same thing as the walls. The walls glowed with soft light, which only showed clearly how trashed everything was.

Still, Jason recognized the large room where Annit led the Yanks. It was the same room he'd seen on Captain Kenara's communication cube. Then the room had been filled with dying colonists, the parents of the fifteen kids who now clustered wonderingly around the Yanks.

Jason looked at a jagged gash in a wall where some machine had been taken out. "How'd they do *that*?"

"Cut it out with a tunable laser saw," Sor said. "What have you been eating since they took the food machines?"

Robbie looked suddenly alert.

"Well," Annit said, "the Panurish—is that what you called them? They never spoke a single word when they came, so we didn't know what they were. Or why they were taking everything."

Sor said, "I've seen pictures of them. They're smaller than we are, right, with sort of pushed-forward faces, thick necks, and reddish hair only on the tops of their heads?"

"That's right," said one of the twins, Mant or Billin; Jason couldn't tell them apart. "They acted like we weren't even here, even when we tried to physically stop them."

"Really? You did?" Sharon said. "What did *they* do?"

"Just pushed us to the floor. Or, rather, their robots did. They came with a lot of robots, and the robots did all the work, cutting everything off the ship and carrying it away and protecting the Panurish. The Panurish just walked around and ignored us."

"Very bad manners," said little Betta.

The fifteen Jump kids all seemed healthy. They were all good-looking, like everyone else Jason had seen in 2336. The youngest, Betta, had been a baby when the Gift Givers landed the *Discovery*; now she was seven. The oldest two, Annit and a boy called Deel, were nineteen. At home in New York, Jason thought, they would be considered adults. But here both Annit and Deel didn't seem any older than him. Maybe because they'd been isolated so long.

Robbie said, "You was talking about food. What do you eat now that the Panurish coves forked your bread-bakes?"

"Oh," Deel said, sounding distracted, "we're using an emergency supply of microdried food-stuffs you just mix with water and—I'm sorry, I don't mean to be rude, but what does it matter what we eat now? You've come to take us back home!"

Come again? Jason looked at Deel's face.

Then at Annit's, and Mant's, and Billin's, and all the others. Their faces shone with joy.

They thought they were going home. Back to Earth, back to whatever family they had left.

And Jason was going to have to tell them different.

"Look, uh, Deel," he said. It was hard to get the words out. "Two things you gotta understand. First, we didn't bring the t-port with us. It was here all the time, about a half-mile away, but it's hard to see if you don't know what you're looking for. Not even the computer on Earth knew it was there until somebody used it a few days ago. The people who sent us here thought the users were Gift Givers, but I guess it was the Panurish instead."

"The reason for the error is clear," da Vinci said. "Wormhole trace radiation wavelengths can—"

"Not now, da Vinci," Jason said quickly. "Cause I still have to tell them the other thing. This t-port only opens for ten minutes at sunset, but last night it didn't open at all. It's gone. Vanished."

"Gone?" Annit said. She turned pale.

"Afraid so."

Betta cried, "The Panurish took it! Like they took everything else!" She started to cry.

Jason thought about that. "What do you think, da Vinci? Is that possible—that the P-dudes just took the t-port?"

"No," da Vinci said. "It's not an object, it's a field. You can't move it."

"Oh," Jason said. "Well, that's a relief, anyway."

"But you could jam the field," da Vinci said, "if you had the right equipment. Then the t-port is still there, but it won't open."

Sor said, "That's probably what happened!"

Jason tried to stay calm. "Then, da Vinci, how do we unjam it?"

"We can't," da Vinci said. "We don't have the equipment. Not with us."

Everyone looked at the robot. Twenty-one pairs of human eyes: fifteen *Discovery* kids and six Yanks, counting Tara. All stuck here on Jump, without a t-port.

Forever?

Maybe forever.

Unless one of them could come up with some plan, some idea. Or unless da Vinci could.

"Da Vinci," Jason said, and the words came thick out of his tight throat, "what do you suggest to get us out of here? Think hard, my man."

"I don't know," da Vinci said. "I don't know of any way we can leave Jump without a t-port."

After that, nobody said anything for a long time.

10

Jason was good. Sharon had to admit that. He didn't let anybody sit around and cry or mope or take out their anger on anybody else. He insisted they all get busy and stay busy.

"Okay, people, we got a lot to do here," Jason said. "We're going start by bedding down in here for the rest of the night and getting some sleep. Then, in the morning, we got to have teams. Five teams of four each, maybe. One team to watch the t-port site all the time, in shifts, in case it appears again. One team to search every crack of this ship for the communication cube, just in case those Panurish *did* miss it somehow. One team to keep things going here, fires and cooking and kid-watching and making stuff we need. Jofrid, I want you to head up that group. And two teams to go look for the Panurish."

Deel said, startled, "Look for the Panurish? We've been avoiding the Panurish!"

"Yeah, well, that was probably good sense," Jason said. "Nasty dudes. But now we know they might have the communication cube, and they probably are jamming the t-port, too. We got to find them and negotiate."

"Negotiate?" Sharon whispered. Negotiate with people—beings, aliens, whoever they were—who wouldn't talk at all, and who fried starships that got in their way? How did you negotiate with aliens like that?

She looked at the *Discovery* kids. Deel and Annit were nineteen years old, and that other girl, the dark-haired beauty, Sharon couldn't remember her name—she was seventeen. How would they take to being bossed around by Jason, who was only about fifteen and had only been on Jump since yesterday?

But Deel and Annit and the dark-haired girl all nodded. Evidently they accepted Jason's leadership. It must be something about him. Either that or the older kids didn't have any ideas of their own and were feeling desperate enough to accept whatever else came along.

Sharon could understand that. She was feeling pretty desperate herself.

Now Jason was putting everybody in teams for tomorrow, with Annit and Deel's help. Sharon made herself speak up. "I'd like to be on the team that looks for the communication cube."

Jason looked at her in surprise. "Not the team that cooks and stuff like that? What about Tara?"

"I can carry her around with me in the ship while I look," Sharon said.

"Okay, if that's what you want," Jason said. "You take the twins and Betta, then, and look for the communications cube."

"But—" Sharon began, but Jason was already

talking about who was on the other teams, and he didn't hear her.

The twins and Betta. Plus Tara, of course. Sharon would be baby-sitting!

Oh, well, she told herself as she settled down to sleep on a bunk that was nothing more than a thin metal shelf protruding from the ship's wall. At least it wasn't only baby-sitting. At least she'd be looking for the communications cube as well.

And she was determined to find it.

The next morning, after a breakfast from ship's stores that tasted wonderful to Sharon, she took her team and started to search the ship. Right away she discovered two things.

First, the *Discovery* had even more compartments than she thought. There had been a couple hundred colonists aboard, but the ship looked as if it could hold many more than that. She asked the twins why.

"I don't remember the landing too well," Mant said, "but Deel told us that people planned to live in the *Discovery* a long time, while they built other stuff. Power plants and things like that. So the *Discovery* was going to be home for maybe a hundred years."

"A hundred *years*?" Sharon said.

"I think that's what Deel said," Mant answered. "Why not?"

"Well—what if their kids, or their kids' kids, wanted to do something different? Build things in a different order, say?"

Mant looked puzzled. "Why would they want to do that?"

Sharon floundered. "Just . . . just because younger generations sometimes want to do things different."

"But if the first plan is the best way, they'd do that," Billin said.

Sharon pondered. In her experience, people didn't choose actions because they were "the best way." People did whatever they pleased. And they didn't trust their parents to make important choices for them. Certainly Sharon wouldn't trust her mother to make choices about her future.

2336 was a stranger place than she'd imagined.

"But," Billin said, sounding very grown up, "you could certainly be right, Sharon."

And that was the second thing she'd learned so far this morning: the twins were polite. Like everybody else in 2336, apparently. The ten-year-old boys Sharon was used to were not usually polite, and she found Mant and Billin a little unnerving. They looked like any boys who had just crawled out from under a dirty bunk, with dust curls on their clothes and smudges of dirt on their faces and their hair standing straight up. But they weren't like the kids she'd known. Mant and Billin—and all the others on Jump—had lost their parents and all other adults, and for six years they'd lived on an isolated planet with other children. Did the twins remember their parents? Did they still miss them? Sharon didn't want to ask, in case it made them sad.

Instead she said, "Well, we've finished this section. Let's try the next one."

"Can I carry Tara?" Betta asked eagerly.

Betta loved having the baby around, Sharon could see. Suddenly Betta wasn't the youngest, the "baby" herself.

"Sure," Sharon said. Betta picked up Tara and staggered with her to the next section of the ship.

The twins crawled under more bunks while Sharon searched through the tangle of objects on the floor, knocked there by the Panurish in their thieving raid.

A hairbrush. It looked just like Sharon's own brush at home. Weird to think that some things didn't change even in three hundred and fifty years.

A long green ribbon.

A stuffed bunny, not made of cloth but still very soft, for a baby to play with.

A vase made of painted metal. A few dead flowers dropped from it.

A plate made of plastic. Or something like plastic.

A blanket.

"Nothing here," Billin said. "Let's go on to the cargo hold. There's *tons* of things there."

"Okay," Sharon said. "But first, look at this vase. It's got flowers in it, and they've only been dead a few days. Who put them here?"

Mant said, "Oh, this was Annit's room, until the Panurish came and we all started sleeping together in the big lounge. I guess the flowers were hers. She liked that vase."

"No wonder," Sharon said. The vase was beautiful. Made of a heavy metal with a dull gleam, it curved in ways that made her hands want to stroke it. The vase looked . . . *lasting*, somehow. Like it would never wear out, never break. It reminded her of something . . . what?

English class. That was it. That poem she'd been the only one in the class to like: "Ode on a Grecian Urn," by Keats. The vase in that poem, too, was supposed to last forever. How did it go?

"When old age shall this generation waste,
Thou shalt remain, in midst of other woe . . ."

Only the Grecian vase had pictures on it, of a wedding party and musicians and trees. This had only an abstract design of broken lines, in black paint. The Grecian vase sounded prettier.

"Hey, Sharon, are you coming to the cargo bay?" Billin called.

"Coming," she said. She took the vase with her. If Annit could put flowers in it, so could she. Maybe it would cheer people up if they didn't find the communication cube and the t-port.

No, that was stupid. If they didn't find the t-port, nothing would cheer people up. Certainly not a bunch of flowers. *Get real*, she told herself, and followed Billin to the cargo bay.

"What's that?" Jofrid said, pushing her hair off her face. The day was warm, and she'd been bending over a fire made on the ground just outside the open main door of the *Discovery*. Delicious smells floated in the air.

"It's a vase," Sharon said.

"What's that?"

They must not have vases in medieval Iceland. "A thing to put flowers in, Jofrid. To look pretty."

"Oh," Jofrid said. "Are you hungry?"

"Starved." It was true. Searching all over the ship was hard work, especially carrying Tara. Jofrid didn't ask if Sharon and her team had found the cube. *She knows I'd mention it if we had,* Sharon thought.

"This is strange food," Jofrid said. "You don't pick it, or hunt it, or prepare it. You heat water and add this magic powder, and soup appears. Do you think it's black magic? Those twin boys have already eaten it, but some black magics take much time to work."

"I'm sure it's okay," Sharon said. It just looked freeze-dried to Sharon.

She ate a bowl of the soup; it tasted wonderful. Tara liked it, too, eating a big bowl and then falling asleep on a blanket in the shade of the ship.

Sharon said to Jofrid, "Where's the rest of your housekeeping team?"

"I sent them to gather fruit and potatoes and anything else we can test to eat. I wanted them to set snares for pigbirds, too, but they will not. They're all *Discovery* people." Jofrid sighed.

"Sharon, we shouldn't just rely on these magic food powders. If we do . . ." Her voice trembled, but she recovered herself and went on. "If we do in the end stay here forever, the powders will be used up someday. We must prepare. We must learn to farm. Find some animal that will give milk. Make a real homestead here."

Sharon knew Jofrid was right, but she couldn't bear to think about it. Stay here forever! Instead she said, "Did you tell Jason this? What does he say?"

"He says we must all learn to play football."

"*What?*"

"Yes," Jofrid said, putting twigs onto the fire. "I said that football would not feed us. Jason said it would make us all, colonists and Yanks, into a true team. Once we are a true team, then we will be able to solve the problems of building a homestead."

"*Football?*"

"Also something called basketball."

"You know what I think, Jofrid?" Sharon said.

"What?"

"I think it's a guy thing."

Jofrid giggled. Then Sharon found herself giggling, too. Jofrid said, "They are strange, men. I am handfast, you know."

"What's that mean?"

"Betrothed, the English priest called it. To be married. To Thorfinn Egilson. We will marry in the summer."

"Engaged! But how old are you, Jofrid?"

"Fourteen. I should have been handfast two years ago, but . . . but . . ." Suddenly Jofrid looked like she would cry.

Sharon got up and put her arm around the girl. Jofrid came only up to Sharon's shoulders. "But what, Jofrid?"

"But no man asked for me, because I'm not maidenly. I go up to the High Seat and talk to my father before he bids me speak. I say what I think. I look my father's men in the eyes. Until Thorfinn asked for me, I thought I should never marry. And now . . . now . . ."

"Now what?" Sharon said. "What is it?"

The small girl's shoulders shook. "I don't like Thorfinn!"

"Then don't marry him!" Sharon cried. "You shouldn't marry somebody you don't like. Wait for somebody you do like."

Jofrid freed herself from Sharon's arm and straightened up. "I shouldn't talk of it now. If we don't find the magic door, I will not be going home anyway. And it is not your problem, Sharon. Let's talk of something else. You were going to teach me a song, like your skalds recite."

Sharon couldn't sing. She had an awful voice. But she had to do something to distract Jofrid. The metal vase sat on the ground beside the fire.

"Okay, Jofrid, I'll recite a poem we learned in English class. Or part of it, anyway. It's about a vase, only the vase in the poem has pictures of a wedding on it. And the poet thinks that the wedding on the vase is better than the real thing, because on the vase the bride will never get old, and the couple will never fight or get divorced, and the wedding music will go on forever. Listen, it goes like this:

"Heard melodies are sweet, but those unheard
Are sweeter; therefore ye soft pipes, play on;
Not to the . . . something something
  something . . .
Pipe to the spirit ditties of no tone
Fair youth, beneath the trees thou canst not
  leave
Thy song, nor ever can those trees be bare;
Bold lover, never, never canst Thou kiss,

Though winning near the goal—yet do not grieve;
She cannot fade, though thou hast not thy bliss;
Forever wilt thou love, and she be fair!"

"Oh, I like that!" Jofrid said. "Will you teach it to me? Only what does the 'something something something' part mean?"

"That's where I forgot the words," Sharon said apologetically. "Maybe they'll come to me."

"The part about 'winning near the goal'—is that the same manner of goal that Jason talks about in football?"

"Well, no," Sharon said.

"What makes the two goals different?"

"Well, let me think." Sharon was feeling confused. In English class there was Mr. Daniels to explain hard meanings.

Jofrid said, "Is the goal in the poem the same as a 'basketball goal,' then? Jason says I must make a basket out of vines for that goal."

"No, it—" But Sharon didn't get a chance to explain. At that moment the girls heard shouting. The next minute the eight kids who had gone to find the Panurish came over the closest hill, some running, some shouting.

"Sor is carrying someone!" Jofrid cried. "Oh, he's carrying Robbie, and Robbie looks . . . oh, Sharon! I think Robbie is dead!"

11

At first, Jason thought they'd lucked out big-time.

Early in the morning he left the *Discovery* with two teams of four kids each, to look for the Panurish. Over a quick breakfast Jason had instructed his seven teammates about what they were supposed to do. He'd lain awake a long time last night, sweating it until he had a good plan.

"It's going to take a while till we find the P-dudes, because they'll be hiding. We'll set off in four directions. Robbie, Wu, Cam, you're the three scouts. If any of you see them first, you *don't* approach alone. Everybody clear on that? You come back to the main group. But if the main group finds 'em, we'll start negotiating, because there'll be enough of us. Got that?"

Everyone nodded. Sor, Robbie, Cam, Deel, Annit, Wu, and Corio. Jason had been careful to learn all their names. Plus, of course, da Vinci.

"If nobody sees the Panurish, then we report back to the ship at high noon, right? And remember, finding them is going to take time."

Then they saw the Panurish ten minutes after leaving the ship.

It was *weird*. The aliens were walking in a straight, tight line like some kind of marching drill. There were eight of them, and beside each Panurish marched a robot. Silently Sor passed a flat thing from his tool pouch to Jason. It turned out to be amazing binoculars, so Jason got to see everything in close-up.

The Panurish were indeed smaller than humans, as Sor said. They had two arms and two legs and a normal-looking body, dressed in clothes that looked like s-suits except they were a dull green. Their heads differed from humans the most: pushed-forward faces, thick necks, and reddish hair only on the tops of their heads.

Sor said, "There's a third eye on the tops of their heads. We think they evolved on a world with lots of flying predators."

"Keep your voice down!" Jason said. "They'll hear you!"

"Oh, they already know we're here, Jason. Their heat-detection equipment will have told them that. It's quite good."

"It is? How do you know?"

"Because it's ours. The third robot in line is carrying it."

Da Vinci said, "I have scanned and analyzed the Panurish robots. They are much more primitive than I am." Jason would swear that da Vinci sounded pleased.

"Yeah?" Jason said. "What can they do? Can they attack?"

"Oh, almost certainly. But each 'bot can probably carry out only one main function at a time, plus simple locomotion. Those robots are for protection."

"Bodyguards," Jason said. He looked closely at the robots, cylinders with long flexible tentacle arms, like da Vinci. But the Panurish robots had no head, which da Vinci did. Instead, they had broad flat tops on which they carried more stuff than would fit into their arms.

Jason said, "What else can you tell from your scans, da Vinci?"

"Nothing else."

"Well, what are they *doing*?"

"I have no idea," da Vinci said.

"Annit? Deel?"

Deel said, "We don't know. We've only seen them once, remember, when they raided the ship."

"Sor?"

"Little is known about the Panurish's habits. But maybe they're exercising. Or playing a game of some sort."

It didn't look like much of a game to Jason. March along, don't talk, don't look to either side. How would you know who won?

"Or," da Vinci said, "it could be a religious ritual. Many cultures have those."

"Well, whatever it is, we're going to follow it," Jason said. "All the way back to their base, so we know where it is. Then before they go in, we're going to start negotiating."

"About this negotiation," Deel said. " 'Negotiating' usually means that both parties offer something the other wants. We know what the Panurish have that we want: the communication cube. But why should they give it up?"

"Because they don't know what it looks like. So we're going to convince them it looks like a different thing, and we really want that *other* thing. Then we take the cube in default."

Corio said, "I don't understand."

Jason turned to him to explain. "It's a fake-out, see? Like suppose you got a cool sweater I really want. I act like the sweater's nothing, but I drool over your backpack and eye it a lot and act like I'm really into that backpack. I offer to trade it for something. You say no. I offer more and more. You keep refusing. Then finally I act all disappointed, but by that time I had a chance to notice what you like about the stuff I'm offering to trade. Pretty soon *you're* trying to make a trade with *me*. Finally, acting a bit down, I agree to trade what you like for the sweater. Then I slink off with what I really wanted, only you let it go 'cause you never caught on that I wanted it. See?"

"No," Corio said, looking confused.

"Well, you'll see it when we do it."

"But," Corio asked, "why should the Panurish trade with us for anything? They can just *take* whatever they want. We don't have any weapons left."

"Well, maybe we got stuff they can't take."

Corio was persistent. "Like what?"

"I don't know *yet*," Jason said, with careful patience. "Don't you see? We gotta wait to see how it goes down."

Corio was quiet, but he still looked confused. The others didn't look too convinced about Jason's plan, either. Well, nobody else was coming up with a better one! Sometimes you just had to play it by ear.

"Come on," he said to everybody, "let's go. We'll follow the Panurish to wherever they live. That's step one."

The Panurish turned out to live fairly close: only about a mile from the *Discovery*. Their ship was much smaller than the human ship. In fact, it barely looked big enough for the eight Panurish, eight robots, and some basic supplies. Well, that made sense, Jason thought. It wasn't a colony ship, built to bring whole families to a new planet and sustain them while they built a town. The Panurish vessel was just a pirate ship. Yes, that's exactly what it was: a pirate ship, raiding and stealing other people's stuff and then taking it home with them.

Except—how *were* they going to take it home? All the high-tech equipment from the *Discovery* was piled in a humongous heap beside the Panurish ship. The heap was taller than the ship, and wider. It would never ever fit inside.

"Da Vinci," Jason said, "tell me how the t-port . . . no, wait, not now. We got to start talking to the Panurish before they go inside their ship."

Jason swallowed hard. This was it, then. He was going to talk to aliens. He hoped they wouldn't fry him on the spot.

"Okay, team," he said to the seven kids with him. "You know what to do."

Cam and Corio moved as far away from the Panurish ship as they could get and still see what was happening. If there was violence, they'd run back to the *Discovery* to report it. Deel, Robbie, and Sor, the back-up crew, stayed in the middle ground. And Jason, Annit, Wu, and da Vinci walked toward the aliens.

"Hey," Jason said. "How you doin'?"

Not that he expected the Panurish to understand English. But he did expect them to stop, look at him, say something in their own language. They didn't. They kept on walking toward their ship as if the humans didn't exist.

"Don't go inside," Jason said. "We want to talk." He pantomimed sitting down, talking.

The Panurish kept walking past.

"Hey, hello. My name is Jason. Jason, me." He pointed to his chest.

The Panurish reached the pile of stolen equipment and started looking through it, bit by bit, holding each piece close to one of the robots.

Da Vinci said softly, "They're looking for the communication cube again. That robot is doing sensor scans for anything that looks like a communication program."

Annit said, "It's going to take them a long time. Every piece of equipment they stole has some kind of communication programming inside it, including the toys."

"Yeah, well, we need a communication program with *us*," Jason said. He was getting annoyed. It was creepy to feel like you didn't even exist. "Hey, Panurish! Will you answer if I yell!"

The Panurish didn't answer.

Jason started forward. Da Vinci said quickly, "Stop. I don't know what the range is to set off the bodyguard robots. But don't get any closer."

"Okay," Jason said, frustrated. "Then *you* try. See if their robots will talk to you."

Da Vinci went very still. After a minute Jason

said, "Oh, man he's gone into contemplation again!"

"No, I don't think so," Annit said. "I think he's just trying all communication channels, including ones we can't detect. Wait just a . . . there, he's done."

Da Vinci said, "The Panurish robots are all functional. They detect my signals. But they will not respond."

Now what? Jason thought. How did you communicate with beings that wouldn't talk to you, that you couldn't physically approach, and that didn't acknowledge your existence?

You threw something at them. Something friendly. Jason took some of Jofrid's vine-rope from off his belt. He bent down to gather some of the purple groundcover, wadded it up tight, and wrapped the rope around and around.

"What's that?" Annit said.

"A football."

"A what?"

"Watch," Jason said. "Thirty-three, sixteen, forty-two, *hike!*" And he threw the ball in a sweet high pass toward the pile of stolen equipment.

Almost faster than his eyes could follow, one of the Panurish robots swiveled around. A thin beam of light shot out from its body and hit the football. It fell to the ground as a blackened, burnt cinder.

No Panurish even appeared to notice.

Annit looked at the fried "football." Finally she said, "It didn't work."

"I *know* it didn't work!" Jason said. "And I'm

fresh out of ideas! You got a better . . . Robbie! No!"

Too late. Robbie, who was supposed to be waiting safely in the middle distance, was crawling through the groundcover, low to the ground, toward the far side of the Panurish ship. He must have made a wide circle and sneaked up from the rear. Now he was almost next to the pile of stolen equipment, reaching out one grubby hand to do what he did best, steal things—only Robbie didn't know about the bodyguard robots! He didn't know what the Panurish were like. He thought that because no Panurish or Panurish robot had appeared to notice him, they didn't know he was there.

"Robbie! No!" Jason screamed.

Too late. Robbie's hand and part of his arm were inside the invisible robot range. A beam of light shot out.

Robbie screamed and jerked backward. Still screaming, he writhed on the ground. Jason and Annit, and then Deel and Sor from farther away, ran in a wide circle around the Panurish to get to him.

By the time they did, Robbie had stopped screaming.

"He's dead!" Annit cried.

"No, he just fainted," Jason said, kneeling beside Robbie. "We have to—Sor, not *now*!" For Sor had gone into his usual wimp act at the sight of violence: turning pale and looking like he might throw up. And now Annit and Corio were doing it, too. What a team!

Carefully Jason picked Robbie up. The nineteenth-century kid was so small and light—

didn't they have any bones back then? He was still breathing.

"Let's get him to the ship," Jason said. "Come on!"

Deel said, "But the Panurish took all the medical equipment!"

Jason almost groaned aloud. Instead he said, "Jofrid. She knows a lot of pre-tech stuff. Maybe she'll know what to do! Unless you do, da Vinci?"

"Put cold water on the burn," da Vinci said, which was no help at all because they didn't have any cold water. So Jason started off at a run. The others trailed behind more slowly.

Jason looked back only once. The Panurish were still scanning and taking apart the stolen equipment, just as if nothing had happened, just as if the humans had never been there at all.

Jofrid did know what to do for Robbie. She made a paste from water combined with some herbs in a pocket of her green wool dress and spread it on the burned hand. Then she bandaged the hand with strips from an old blanket. She also gave Robbie something from her pockets to make him sleep.

But Jason couldn't sleep, not even after all the others had dozed off inside the locked-up *Discovery*. Jason lay awake, tossing and turning.

The day had been pretty much a disaster. They'd found the Panurish, sure. But they didn't have the communication cube. They didn't have the t-port back. They didn't have a clue how to negotiate with the Panurish.

And Jason didn't have any more ideas about what to do next.

Sharon wanted to see the Panurish for herself.

She sat on a big rock beside the spring. It was early afternoon of a soft sunny day, with a light lemony-smelling wind. At her feet, Tara played with a soft toy from the *Discovery*. Sharon watched the baby and thought about aliens.

Six days had gone by, and everybody in the *Discovery* had seen the Panurish except her. First the older kids had gone to try to negotiate. That hadn't worked. The Panurish never once even seemed to notice that the humans were there.

But the aliens didn't attack again, either. As long as the humans stayed at least forty feet away from Panurish, robots, ship, and pile of stolen stuff, it was perfectly safe to watch them. So then the younger kids got to go have a look, even seven-year-old Betta. Jason had watches on the aliens all day and all night, in shifts, in case they did anything different, which so far they hadn't.

Everybody was on the watch list except Sharon. She had to baby-sit Tara. Jason wouldn't spare da Vinci for baby-sitting, because "if something big breaks, we'll need da Vinci."

Well, that made sense, but still, Sharon really wanted to see the aliens. Why shouldn't she? She could take Tara with her. It was perfectly safe, that had been proven over and over during the last six days. She wouldn't get very close. And so many feet had trekked over the hills to the alien ship that a path was worn in the groundcover. She wouldn't get lost.

"What are you doing?" Mant asked, walking toward her.

"Thinking," Sharon said.

"That's nice," Mant said politely. "May I ask what you're thinking about?"

He sounded so grown-up that Sharon had to smile. She liked the twenty-fourth-century kids. They were all so gentle and polite.

"I'm thinking about the Panurish," she told Mant.

He nodded. "Jason sent me to get you."

"Jason's back?" He had gone to see if the t-port site had changed in any way. He looked every day. It never changed.

"Yes, he's back," Mant said. "And so is Jofrid's expedition."

"Did they find anything new to eat?"

"I don't know. I hope so."

Mant grinned; he loved the meals Jofrid prepared. A routine had developed about food. Sor tested everything in his edibility machine, and then Jason sent people to gather more of whatever was edible so they wouldn't have to use up too much of the *Discovery*'s stores.

Jason was turning into a good leader. He had

efficient teams for watching the Panurish, for gathering and cooking food, for staking out the t-port, for brainstorming ideas on what to do next. When all the work was done, he even built what he called "team spirit."

"Oh, no," Sharon said. "Not more football."

"I get to be quarterback," Mant said importantly. "Come on, Sharon."

"Mant, I hate football!"

Mant looked shocked. He, along with most of the boys, had taken to Jason's football lessons like a bird to air. Some of the girls, too, loved to play. Annit did, and Cam. But not Sharon. Mant's announcement decided for her. She would take Tara and go look at the Panurish.

"Tell Jason I went for a walk."

She picked up Tara, who was in a good mood, settled the baby on her hip, and followed the path over the low hills to the alien camp. When she arrived, she stayed a safe distance away, squinting through the lemony air at the aliens leaving their ship.

Why, the Panurish were so small! They were kids, after all—she remembered Dr. Cee saying that only Panurish kids could teleport, just like humans—but even for kids they looked little. How old were they?

Sharon walked closer. On the far side of the camp, sitting on a hill well outside the forty-foot attack range, were the two humans on watching shift, Wu and Alli. Beside their tiny ship the Panurish lined up in a very straight row, a robot last in line. They started walking toward her.

Sharon's heart beat fast. Were they attacking? But then she remembered Jofrid telling her about this. Several times a day the Panurish went marching around the hills for about half an hour, in a different direction each day. Nobody knew if this was exercise, reconnaissance, a religious ritual, or whatever. But they just marched in a straight line for fifteen minutes, turned around, and marched back. They never stopped, never changed direction, never looked to the left or right. All Sharon had to do was get out of their way.

She scurried to one side, then cautiously turned and looked back.

The Panurish robot, at the end of the line, didn't look at all like da Vinci. It looked more like a . . . a *suitcase*. Yes, a suitcase with rounded sides and a perfectly flat top, floating along a few inches above the ground.

The aliens marched past her like soldiers on parade. Just as the other humans had all said, they ignored her utterly. Sharon started to breathe normally.

Until, suddenly, the line of Panurish stopped and looked at her.

Sharon froze. This wasn't supposed to happen! And then something even weirder occurred: the Panurish all bent toward her, like they were bowing. But it wasn't a bow. They bent over and each one fixed its third eye, the one on the top of their heads and surrounded by a ring of reddish hair, directly on Sharon.

She was so frightened it took her a minute to realize that the Panurish *weren't* actually looking at her.

They were looking at Tara.

The baby was delighted. She clapped her little hands, giggled, and squirmed to get down. She wanted to crawl towards the interesting people who were looking at her.

Sharon clutched the baby hard, and ran. She was afraid to look back over her shoulder. If the aliens came after her, they could probably move faster than she. Tara felt heavier and heavier. How could Sharon outrun them, the camp was so far away, she was panting already . . .

Something pulled up next to her. The Pan-urish robot!

Sharon screamed. The robot took no notice. It ran—or rather floated—right beside her, matching her pace effortlessly. And then tentacles snaked out of the robot's side and reached for Tara.

"No!" Sharon screamed. "No, no!" She stopped running and tried to beat off the robot. But it was too strong for her. Gently and impersonally it peeled back her arms and took Tara from her. The baby laughed, thinking it was a game.

"Give her back!" Sharon cried. But instead the robot started to move away, slowly, holding Tara as if he wasn't sure how much she could be jostled.

With tottering steps—her knees felt like water—Sharon kept up with the robot. She grabbed at Tara, but the baby was wrapped in the robot's flexible tentacles and Sharon couldn't get her free. What was this thing going to do with Tara? What if it suddenly fried her?

"Stop! Stop!" Sharon yelled. The robot took no notice. It began to move slightly faster. Frantic now, Sharon did the only thing she could think of—she jumped on top of the robot's flat upper surface.

Instantly the robot stopped. It untangled one long arm from Tara, balancing her with the other, and reached over itself to push Sharon off. Immediately Sharon reached forward herself and pulled at Tara, now held by only one tentacle. The robot tightened its grip on the baby, and Tara started to whimper. It didn't like that; it let Sharon go and returned to holding Tara with two gentle tentacles.

They stayed like that for a moment, the three of them: the robot still, the baby whimpering, and Sharon helplessly riding an alien . . . *thing*. She could feel her heart hammering in her chest. What was the robot going to do next? What was *she* going to do next? Oh God, if it hurt Tara . . .

The robot started to tilt.

Sharon felt herself sliding off. Instantly she threw her arms around the suitcase-like body of the robot and hung on. The robot shook her a bit, but not too hard. Maybe it didn't want to shake up Tara? What did it *want* with Tara?

The robot stopped shaking and straightened up. Sharon still hung on. After a moment, it resumed its slow, careful walk back toward the line of waiting aliens.

It was going to give Tara to the aliens!

Sharon groped frantically around the edges of the robot, looking for . . . what? Something, anything! Her trembling hand found a series of bumps. Sensors, maybe? Da Vinci had sensors for heat, motion, sight . . . *Sight*! That was it!

Her groping hand found the optical sensor that let the robot see forward. It protruded out from the suitcase's front, like a single headlight, just to the right of where Tara was pressed against the metal skin. Maybe, Sharon thought wildly, if she could cover the optical sensor, the robot couldn't go forward. She put a hand over the sensor.

The robot stopped. It had worked! But then Sharon's hand started to burn. The sensor was getting hot to burn off whatever was obstructing it.

Sharon yanked away her hand before the heat got too intense. What now? Oh, somebody *please help me* . . .

But there was no one except herself. What else could she do to cover the optical sensor? She spit into her hand and rubbed the spit all over the sensor. Even before she removed her hand, she could feel the heat start. The robot burned off the spit as easily as a hot frying pan burning off drops of water.

What wouldn't it burn off? Anything?

The robot was getting closer to the line of waiting aliens.

Frenziedly Sharon put one hand in the pocket of her s-suit. Her fingers touched a pretty stone Jofrid had given her, plus some things for Tara that had been in her coat pocket when she left Earth. A teething ring, a broken string of beads, a tube of Desenex.

Desenex.

Sharon pulled out the tube of white, sticky, pasty stuff intended to be smeared on a baby's bottom to cure diaper rash. Balancing on the slowly moving robot's flat top, she squirted a big fistful of the goop into her other hand and smeared it onto the optical sensor. Her hand burned and she yanked it away.

The robot stopped moving. Whatever chemicals Desenex was made of, they didn't burn off!

The robot started to turn sideways. Quickly Sharon smeared more Desenex on the optical sensors on the other three sides. The robot stopped dead. It was blind.

Sharon slid off and reached for Tara. But the robot still held her firm. Then it loosened one tentacle from the baby and reached back toward itself to wipe off the Desenex.

Sharon didn't hesitate. She yanked at Tara so hard that the baby screamed. The robot let go of Tara. While the robot wiped the gooey paste off its tentacles, Sharon started running. She knew in a moment the robot would be able to see again. Sure enough, the Panurish robot started after her.

Sharon ran clumsily, her heart pounding. Just ahead was one of the fresh-water springs that seemed to be everywhere on Jump. All that underground water must nourish the thick purple groundcover. This spring was bigger than the others; it had formed a pool as big as a small pond.

Without thinking, Sharon jumped into the water.

She waded toward the center and crouched down as low as she could, until only her head and Tara's were above water. *Stupid, stupid . . .* why would a little water stop a robot?

But it did.

The robot stopped at the edge of the pond and reached its tentacles as far as they could go. They fell just short of reaching Tara. The creature walked around the pond, trying every few feet to extend its tentacles out over the water and grab back Tara. But each time, Sharon moved a bit in the opposite direction, and the tentacles were just a bit too short.

Why didn't it go into the water? Sharon wondered wildly. Then an answer came to her. Sor had said the pigbirds had evolved in a lighter gravity than Earth's, and so that's why they could run faster than animals just as heavy-looking could on Earth. Maybe the Panurish had evolved on a planet without much water in open, above-ground bodies. So they couldn't swim, and they didn't build their robots to swim, either . . .

The robot kept circling the pond, but no matter how many times it tried, it couldn't reach Tara and Sharon. And the Panurish themselves didn't approach the pond at all. Well, that fit, Sharon thought; they never came near humans or let humans come near them if robots could do the job. Maybe they were cowards?

Tara, cold from the water, started wailing and kicking. Sharon paid her no attention. She kept both of them submerged to their chins while their lips turned blue. She wasn't leaving until the robot gave up and went away.

Eventually, it did.

Even then, Sharon waited in the pond as long as she could stand it. When she was so cold she thought she'd die, she finally came out and ran, on stiff and trembling legs, back to the *Discov-*

ery. Nobody stopped her. The aliens and their robot had apparently marched away.

She panted up to Jofrid and Betta, outside the ship. Betta tended a small fire. Robbie lay on the ground while Jofrid spread some sort of medicinal paste on his burned hand and put fresh bandages over it.

"Sharon! You're all wet!" Betta said. "What happened?"

"The . . . the Panurish . . . They tried to take Tara . . ."

"Take Tara!" Jofrid cried.

Robbie sat straight up on the grass. "You gammoning us, miss?"

"Yes. They . . . they stopped marching, bent over to look through that third eye, and looked straight at us. Then they tried to grab her!"

"Sit by the fire," Jofrid said. "Oh, you're freezing! Tara, too! Tell what happened."

Sharon did, gradually warming up as she sat by the fire. Jofrid got Tara out of her sopping clothes and wrapped her in a blanket; the baby stopped crying. When Sharon was done talking, little Betta said, "But why did the aliens want Tara?"

Jofrid looked thoughtful. "Perhaps because they've never seen a baby before. The oldest colony child is you, Betta, and you're already seven. You no longer look like a baby. You walk, talk, show fear . . . was Tara afraid of the Panurish, Sharon?"

"No," Sharon said. "Not at first. She thought they were great. Clapped her hands and gurgled and wanted to get down and go see."

"Well, perhaps that behavior made them curious," Jofrid said.

"They haven't been curious about any of our other behavior," Betta pointed out.

Robbie said, "It bams me what their lay really is. Peculiar coves, them."

Sharon asked. "They—hey, what's all that noise on the other side of the ship?"

"Basketball," Robbie answered.

"Jason's teaching everybody," Betta said. "Robbie can't play until his hand is better. Jason put up a hoot made of vines."

"A hoop," Sharon corrected automatically. "What happened to football?"

"Jason said the season's over. Now it's basketball season. He made two teams, the Knicks and the Wizards. What's a knick?"

"I don't know," Sharon said. She was still cold and scared. Even so, it registered in one part of her mind that all the furious shouting didn't sound much like a basketball game.

It wasn't. Jason came charging around the corner of the huge starship, followed by every other human except Wu and Alli. Everybody shouted at everybody else. Jason ran straight up to Robbie, who sat on the ground next to the fire.

"You mangy little runt! What have you been doing with those pigbirds?"

Robbie stood up slowly. Sharon saw his eyes glitter. He said to Jason, "Why, guv'nor, Robbie's been snaring the pigbirds for Jofrid to cook. You know that."

"And what have you been doing with 'em before you brought them to Jofrid? Answer me that?"

"Why, nothing, guv'nor."

"Sor says otherwise. Sor, tell him what you found!"

Sor stepped forward. He was pale, with a look in his eyes that Sharon had learned to recognize. All the colony kids got it in the presence of violence. It was a sort of squeamish distaste, coupled with outrage that anyone could resort to such uncivilized behavior, much less enjoy it. It was the underlying reason Sor hated Robbie so much, although Sharon sensed that Sor was also sickened by his own hatred. Probably he thought hatred was a form of violence, too.

Sor said, in a controlled voice, "I was on patrol with Billin, searching for more edible plants. We walked two point six miles north-northeast from the *Discovery*. And we found a place beside a spring where somebody made a pen out of strong sticks tied with vines. In the pen was a pigbird. It had gashes and pulled-out feathers, as if it had been fighting. Beside the pen was a circle of bare dirt, with two stakes in it. The stakes had ropes on them, and the ropes were bloody. Inside the circle was another pigbird, still tied, all bloody. It was dead."

"You been cockfighting!" Jason said. "You been making those pigbirds fight so you can get a champion and run gambling games! Haven't you?"

Robbie said nothing. But his eyes still glittered.

Sor said in a quiet, deadly voice, "Who did you think would come to your barbaric games? Who did you think would make bets? None of us want to watch cruelty and death to animals for your sick sport."

Robbie said, "You want them Panurish to talk to us, don't you?"

Jason gasped. "The *Panurish*?"

Robbie held up his burned hand. "The Panurish roasted Robbie's hand, didn't they? Looked interested while they did it, too. You didn't see that, guv'nor, nor did you, Sor. Too busy yelling at Robbie. But I saw. They're right and proper bloody, them Panurish, and they got the rumgumption to appreciate a good cockfight. You see if they don't. They'll talk to us yet."

Jason and Sor stared at Robbie. So did Sharon. She felt sick at the thought of making pigbirds fight to the death for fun. But . . . what if Robbie was right? What if a cockfight would make the Panurish willing to negotiate?

Sor said to Robbie, "You are disgusting."

Robbie said to Jason, "You up for giving it a try, guv'nor? Wager with the Panurish, winner gets the t-port back so's we can go home?"

Jason said, "No. Yes. I don't know. I need to think about it. We need to talk about it more."

Sor said, "Jason! No good ever came from evil behavior."

Jason ran his hand through his tightly curled hair. Sharon had noticed that he did that when he was really stressed out. Jason said again, "I need to think about it."

" 'Course you do, guv'nor," Robbie said, at his most cheerful.

Jofrid said, "All important matters are better for careful weighing."

Jason smiled at her gratefully. But all he said was, "You know it, babe."

Sharon still sat close to the fire. Jason hadn't even noticed that she was wet from head to toe. Young Billin dropped on the ground next to her, and she forced herself to pay attention to him. "How was the basketball game?"

"Awesome!" Billin said. He must have learned the word from Jason. "I made a free throw!"

"But we won!" Cam said.

Billin bristled at her. "The game wasn't over yet! We were interrupted!"

"But our team was ahead," Cam said. "Way ahead."

Sor, of their century but older by several years, looked troubled. "Surely the point of competition in a game is fun, not boasting over winning."

"Yeah, Sor's right," Jason said. "You supposed to act cool when you win, Cam. You're like, 'You fought a good game, dudes. Better luck next time.' That's class."

Cam looked puzzled at this, but she nonetheless nodded.

"Awesome," Billin said.

He loped off, followed by all the others except Jofrid. Jofrid squeezed Sharon's hand. "You're all right now, my friend, and so's Tara. All is well that ends well. And you outwitted the Panurish robot. You showed what Sor calls grit, Sharon."

Sharon thought about it. Was that "grit"? Smearing diaper-rash goo on a robot's optical sensors and then hiding neck-deep in a pond? It seemed a strange definition.

But maybe Jofrid was right. Maybe she had shown grit. She, Sharon Myers.

She squeezed Jofrid's hand back. Suddenly Sharon felt much, much better.

In the middle of the night, Sharon woke up. Something wasn't right. She didn't know what, but she sensed it.

The colony kids had all gone back to their own quarters once they were sure the Panurish had taken everything they wanted and weren't coming back. The Yanks had chosen rooms and roommates from among all the extra space. Sharon and Jofrid shared, sleeping on two comfortable lower bunks across from each other, with a crib for Tara in the middle. Now Sharon groped for the place on the wall to make it glow with dim light. The light went on and Sharon looked around.

Tara was gone.

13

They searched the whole ship. Tara wasn't in it.

Jason didn't want to admit it, but he was scared. How could the Panurish have gotten inside a locked ship and stolen the baby? Did that mean they could get inside any time they wanted?

"Okay," he said to Billin and Betta, who were on his search team. The teams were a mess, just thrown together with shouted commands as people woke up. There'd been no time to plan, no time to think. The important thing had been just to get everybody looking for Tara—who wasn't anywhere.

"Okay, Billin, Betta. Go find everybody and tell them to meet in the center hall. We need to get organized. Go!"

The two colony kids scampered off, looking as scared as Jason felt. That stupid baby! Jason had known she'd be trouble! Still, she was only a little baby, and he didn't want anything bad to happen to her. What did the humans really know about the Panurish, anyway? What if they *ate* babies?

He better find Sharon. God, he hoped she wasn't hysterical. A hysterical girl was the last thing Jason needed right now.

Sharon wasn't hysterical. She stood in the center hall, between Jofrid and Sor, looking pale as new paper. But she wasn't screaming or crying or fainting, for which Jason was grateful.

"Look, Sharon, it's going to be all right. We'll find Tara. We'll . . ." He had to stop because of all the noise. Sharon might be quiet, but Billin and Betta and Mant went tearing through the hall on their way to the back of the *Discovery*, screaming, "Jason says come to the hall! JASON SAYS EVERYBODY COME TO THE HALL NOW! JASON SAYS EVERYBODY—"

In a few minutes everyone had arrived, dressed in pajamas and day clothes and s-suits, looking uncombed and unwashed and scared. Jason tried to make his voice calm.

"Okay, people. What we got to do now is—"

"Robbie isn't here," Sor said. His voice sounded weird.

Jason looked around the hall, counting fast. Eight, nine, ten . . . eighteen, nineteen . . . It was true. Everyone was present except Robbie.

And Tara.

A cold, awful feeling slid down his spine.

Sor said, still in that same strange voice, flat and furious at the same time, "He took her. Robbie took Tara and left the ship."

Jason burst out, "Why? That doesn't make sense!"

Sharon started to tremble. She gasped, "The P-P-Panurish, they t-tried to take Tara—"

"What?" Jason said. "Sor, what's she talking about? Jofrid, do you know?"

Jofrid answered. Now she was as pale as Sharon. The other kids all crowded around to listen as Jofrid said, "Sharon told us yesterday. Robbie was there. It was by the fire, in the afternoon—"

"*What* was?" Jason roared. "Will somebody please tell me what you're talking about?"

Jofrid said, "In the afternoon. Sharon went for a walk to see the Panurish, and she took Tara. The Panurish were making a march. But they all stopped walking and looked at Tara, and then their robot tried to grab her, but Sharon got away."

"Grab Tara?" Deel said intently. "You mean, they actually paid attention to Sharon and Tara?"

"More than just 'paid attention,' " Jofrid said. She told the whole story, ending with, "Sharon told me all about it by the fire, and Robbie heard, he was there because I was bandaging his hand!"

Jason said, "Why wasn't I told about all this?"

Jofrid said, "It was right before your anger about Robbie making the pigbirds fight. Everything was so noisy . . ." She trailed off and put an arm around her friend. Sharon didn't seem to notice.

Jason didn't know a person could look like Sharon did.

Sor said bitterly, "And so Robbie took Tara to sell to the aliens."

Everybody gaped at him.

Sor continued, "Robbie took the baby to the

Panurish camp to sell, or trade, for the communication cube. I would bet my life on it. He knew Tara was the only human thing of any interest at all to the Panurish, and he has no ethics, no morals, no common humanity. He's trading Tara to them right now."

Then Sharon did scream. A small, despairing scream, even worse than if she had gotten hysterical. Her desperate, giving-up cry said she didn't believe Jason could fix this.

Well, he was at least going to try!

"You don't *know* Robbie took Tara," he said swiftly to Sor, "but he might have, so we gotta check it out. Quick. Maybe he's not even there yet, maybe he just left. Deel and Annit, you're the fastest. Come with me and see if we can catch him. Sor, you stay here and get everybody else organized to—" To do what? "To search other places outside the ship Tara might be. Deel, Annit, come on!"

"I'm coming, too," Sor said. "Wu, you organize the search here."

"I'm coming," Sharon said.

There was no time to argue. Jason ran for everything he was worth toward the Panurish ship, his long legs outdistancing the others. Five moons were up, flooding the path with enough light to run without tripping. Enough light to see even a weasely runt carrying a baby. Jason was all the way to the Panurish camp before he saw Robbie.

Alone. Without Tara.

Robbie took one look at Jason tearing toward him, Deel and Sor and Annit and Wu pounding behind, and Robbie ran. He was fast, but Jason was faster. Jason caught him in a little dell filled with the lemony Jump scent of night-blooming flowers. He grabbed Robbie by the upper arms and almost lifted him off his feet.

"Where is Tara, you bastard? *Where is she?*"

"Now, guv'nor, I just—"

"You just what? *What?!!*"

"Let him answer," Deel said. "Jason, you're hurting him!"

With effort, Jason loosened his grip on Robbie. Sor and Sharon appeared at the top of the nearest hill, running toward them.

"Okay, Robbie," Jason said. "Tell me where Tara is. And make it quick."

"I forked the baby for the good of everybody," Robbie whined. "Them Panurish, they liked the baby, and it's the first thing of ours they did like. So I asked meself, why? 'Cause they want to learn about us, the answer come to me. So I offered 'em a trade—keep the baby for a few days, and we keep all the stuff they already looked through and don't want no more. Maybe in that stuff that there cube-thing—"

Deel said, "You traded *Tara*? And the Panurish agreed to the bargain?"

"Didn't agree to nothin'," Robbie said. "Piked on the bean, they did. Took the baby and locked Robbie out!"

"You—" Jason began, but before he could finish, Sor's voice came from behind them. Sor's voice, but different than Jason had ever heard it. Low, deadly. And Sor didn't look like himself. Gone was the smiling, polite twenty-fourth-century wimp. Sor looked like a man who could kill somebody.

"You sold a human being. You are a despicable piece of garbage and deserve no mercy." Before Jason could stop him, Sor seized Robbie around the neck and dragged him from Jason's grip.

Robbie started to fight. It was like a rabbit fighting a tiger. Sor was a foot taller, stronger, better nourished, and angrier than Jason had ever seen a person get. He started to beat Robbie with hard, deadly punches.

"Stop! Stop!" Annit yelled. "You'll kill him!"

Jason sprang forward and tried to get Robbie out of Sor's grasp. But Sor was unstoppable. Like some great deadly expressionless machine, he kept hitting Robbie no matter how Jason tried to interfere.

"Sharon!" Deel cried. "Tell Sor to stop! He'll listen to you!"

But Sharon said nothing. Suddenly Jason was afraid that Sor *would* kill Robbie. Sor was so outraged at what Robbie had done, so furious and horrified and sickened, that something had snapped in all that polite restraint and Sor . . . my God, Sor might murder the little runt!

Jason made one final desperate lunge to pull Robbie away from Sor. It was the worst thing he could possibly have done.

He got Robbie partially free. Instantly Robbie's unburned left hand darted down and pulled his knife from his boot.

"No!" Jason cried, but it was too late to stop Robbie from lunging with the knife. All Jason had time to do was thrust his own body into the space between the flailing Robbie and the deadly Sor.

He felt the knife slide smoothly into his own side.

The pain was surprising. It started out feeling fiery, a thin burning line in Jason's flesh. Then all at once it turned cold.

"He's fainting," somebody said.

No, I'm not, Jason thought, and then, *Yes, I am.* The last thing he saw was Sor, standing with his head in his hands, moaning, *"What did I do, what did I do?"* Then Jason keeled over and everything went dark.

He revived inside the *Discovery*, under piles of blankets. Jofrid, Cam, and Deel sat beside him.

"He's awake," Cam said.

Jofrid put a cool hand on his forehead. "How do you feel?"

It struck Jason as the dumbest question in the entire world. He was just knifed, Tara was stolen, Sor was bonkers, Sharon was like somebody dead, they were marooned on Jump . . . How should he feel? Give me a break!

But all he said aloud was, "Okay."

"Your wound is slight," Jofrid went on. "The knife was deflected by a rib. The gods smiled on you."

"You fainted from shock," Deel said.

Jofrid said, "I have tended far worse when my father's men returned from going a-viking. You should not pamper yourself."

"Yeah, well, I wasn't planning on no pampering," Jason said. He sat up. At first he was mad at Jofrid's lack of sympathy, but then all at once he was grateful for it. That was the ticket—get on with it, no self-pity. And he wasn't even hurt very bad, she said.

Jason put his hand to his side. He could feel thick bandages, and under them some cooling salve. Probably another one of Jofrid's plant concoctions. Jofrid was a useful person, big-time. Imagine one of his New York babes knowing how to treat him if he got cut. Never happen. All they could do was call 911. Which sure wasn't going to work on Jump.

"Thanks, Jofrid," Jason said. "You're all right, babe."

Jofrid blushed with pleasure.

"But now we got to get back to business. Where's Robbie?"

"Nobody knows," Deel said. "He ran off."

"Where's Sor?"

"With Sharon," Deel said. "They're watching the Panurish ship to see if the aliens bring Tara out. Sharon won't leave there."

"Where's da Vinci?"

"He fell into contemplation last night. Don't you remember?"

No, Jason did not remember. The robot had been with him and Sor when they'd found Robbie's pigbird-fighting setup. After that, Jason had been so furious he hadn't noticed whether da Vinci even raced back with him to the ship. Apparently da Vinci hadn't.

Jason said, "Why did da Vinci fall into contemplation this time? He's seen pigbirds before!"

Deel and Jofrid looked at each other. Finally Deel said, "It was a new alien phenomenon that made da Vinci go contemplative. Robbie."

"*Robbie*? You mean, da Vinci found Robbie so alien he fell into contemplation?"

"Yes," Deel said. "The idea that Robbie would deliberately set up fights among animals . . . it's too alien to da Vinci. It threw off his logic circuits. Remember, my society programmed him, and it's alien to us, too."

"Great," Jason muttered. "A robot that not only goes useless because of alien stuff, but because of some human stuff, too. Just what we need. Who can get him working again?"

"Only Sor," Deel said. "And he won't leave Sharon."

Jason sighed. "What time is it now?"

"Seven in the morning," Deel said.

"I slept all night?"

"I gave you something to make you sleep," Jofrid said calmly. "Something I brought from Iceland in the pockets of my dress."

Jason didn't like the sound of that. She'd knocked him out. What else could she do with the drugs she brought from Iceland? That was one lethal dress. However, this wasn't the time to go into it.

He said to Annit, "Organize some teams to go find Robbie. Tell him nobody will hurt him again, I promise, but I have to talk to him. Okay? And now I'm going to the Panurish ship. I want you, Jofrid, to go with me. Also Deel and Wu. Can I walk okay?"

"You are a man," Jofrid said, which Jason interpreted to mean yes. Or else it meant, *Men walk even if they're injured and can't.* Those Vikings from Jofrid's time must have been some tough dudes.

They set off slowly toward the Panurish ship. Wu carried a basket of food for Sor and Sharon. Deel carried fresh water from the spring. Jason's side hurt, but it was nothing he couldn't handle.

Sor and Sharon sat on the usual watching spot, a hill outside the alien ship, about a hundred yards away. Both of them looked like they'd been through a war.

Jason thought, *I'm the leader. It's up to me to do whatever I can.*

"Sharon? You all right, babe?" Jason asked her.

She didn't even answer. He was going to have to do a whole lot better than that.

Jason sat down on the hill beside her. Wu and Deel put down the food and water, and Jason waved them away. They withdrew a short distance. Jofrid stayed beside Sharon.

Jason said, "Look, Sharon, I'm not going to try to snow you. It's bad that the Panurish have Tara. We don't know what they'll do. But try to remember that very thing—we *don't* know what they'll do. That means they might be treating Tara real good. No, don't look at me like that—it's true. They might like babies, or even worship babies, for all we know. Or they might just be taking good care of her so they can . . ."

Can *what*? Jason was running out of ideas. Then inspiration came to him. "They're probably taking good care of her so they can study how humans grow up."

Sharon said, "Why would they want to know that? They haven't wanted to know anything else about us!"

142

"No, Sharon," Sor said, "Jason might be right. The Panurish want to examine a human, probably. It's always good to know what the competition is made of. But they might be afraid to let us inside their ship, because then we might learn about *them*. But a baby is perfect. They can observe her, and even if we somehow got her back, she wouldn't be able to tell us anything about them because she's too young."

"Do you think so?" Sharon said. She sounded a little more hopeful. "So they'd keep Tara alive to study her better?"

"I'm sure of it!" Jason said heartily. Privately, though, he wondered. What if what the Panurish wanted to know was how a human being looked inside? But if that were so, they'd have captured and dissected one of the *Discovery* kids, and they hadn't.

Sor said, "We'll just sit here and watch, and wait for our chance to get Tara back."

Sharon nodded. Okay, Jason thought: one person feeling better. Now Sor.

"Sharon, could I talk to Sor alone for just a minute? Sor, come over here with me."

They moved sideways along the hill. Sor looked awful: bleary-eyed, hollow-cheeked, pale. Jason plunged right in. "Look, I know you feel bad about beating the shit out of Robbie."

"He deserved it," Sor said, and then, almost immediately, "What am I saying? Violence is never a good way to settle conflict! It solves nothing!"

So that was it, Jason thought. Sor was torn between his emotions and his beliefs. The poor dude was trying to feel two different things at once. What could Jason say to him?

"Listen, Sor," Jason went on. "Personally, I think Robbie had it coming to him. You didn't kill him."

"If it hadn't been for you, I would have," Sor pointed out despairingly. "I would have committed *murder*!"

"Yeah, but you didn't. It worked out okay. And Robbie will be back, bet on it. He's got—" What was that word the twenty-fourth century docs kept saying that the Yanks all had? "He's got *grit*. Robbie will get over this and join the team again. You just stay out of his way, and vice versa, and we'll work it all out, one way or another."

Sor didn't look convinced. Well, why should he? Jason wasn't even convinced by his own words. Work it out *how*? But it was the best he could do at the moment.

He and Sor moved back toward Sharon and Jofrid and sat down. The four of them stared steadily at the Panurish ship. The next move was the aliens'.

Whatever it would be.

14

Nothing happened until noon. Then the Panurish ship opened and a line of the little aliens emerged, in the usual strict formation. Without Tara.

Sharon jumped up. Maybe she could run inside the Panurish ship while the door was open, grab Tara, run out with her . . . But even before she felt Jason grab her hand and pull her back down on the hillside, she knew the idea was dumb. The second she got closer than forty feet, the Panurish robots would fry her.

The aliens started off on their usual inexplicable march, the door to their ship closed, and Sharon sank deeper into despair.

She didn't really believe the Panurish would just study Tara. She'd pretended to believe it, because Jason so clearly wanted her to. But underneath, Sharon was sure they'd do something awful to Tara. Dissect her, eat her . . . Who knew?

Sharon shuddered. But she tried not to lose it completely. If there was any way to get Tara back, she had to stay calm enough to find it.

Calm! It seemed to Sharon she could never

ever be calm again. It seemed like years ago that she'd been talking about calmness with Jofrid, admiring Jofrid's unflappability, teaching Jofrid that Keats poem praising the calmness of the Grecian urn—*"Thou foster child of silence and slow time"* . . .

Sharon buried her head in her hands. Thinking of a stupid poem from English class, at a time like this! What was wrong with her? She needed to focus all her thoughts on getting Tara back.

The problem was, no chance turned up the rest of the day. The Panurish came, the Panurish went, the Panurish examined the huge pile of equipment stolen from the *Discovery*, bit by careful bit. But there was no glimpse of Tara.

At midafternoon, Jason and Jofrid returned to the *Discovery*, then came back a while later carrying bags. Jason, Sharon saw, walked more slowly than usual, his hand clapped against his side where Robbie had knifed him.

"Hey, Sharon, how you doin'?" Jason said kindly.

"We brought you some food," Jofrid said.

"Thanks," Sharon said tonelessly. She knew she wouldn't be able to eat.

Jofrid said, "There will be a sign of Tara soon, Sharon. I am sure of it."

Sharon wished she were as sure. But Jofrid's presence, the presence of a friend, was comforting. Jason, however, had something else on his mind.

"Listen, Sharon," Jason said. "Cam said that when she and Deel were on watch here, they couldn't get as close to the Panurish ship as humans could before. They couldn't sit on their usual watch hill. Did you try to go down any closer to the ship?"

"No," Sharon said. She hadn't moved in hours. But she tried to rouse herself enough to follow what Jason was saying. "What do you mean, they couldn't get as close as before?"

"Something weird stopped them. They didn't know what, but I'm going to find out. Sor, come with me."

"Walk with care," Jofrid warned.

Jason and Sor started down the hill toward the Panurish ship. About sixty feet away from it, they stopped and Jason began to feel the air with the palms of his hands, as if there was an invisible but very solid wall directly in front of him. Sor did the same. They reminded Sharon of those white-faced mimes on TV, silently fingering what nobody else could see. Slowly the two moved in opposite directions along a circular "wall," until they met on the far side of the ship. Then they returned to Sharon and Jofrid. Sweat beaded Jason's forehead.

"Cam was right," Sor said. "There's an invisible fence all around the ship. It must be some sort of electronic field."

"Ask da Vinci," Jofrid suggested.

"Yeah, I will," Jason said. "Sharon, did you see the aliens march out in their straight line this morning?"

"Yes."

"And they just marched on through the electronic fence?"

"I guess so," Sharon said. "They didn't slow down at all."

Jofrid said, "The barrier must be for added protection. They fear us, even though they are so much more heavily armed. Fear is always a weakness, my father says."

Jason said, maybe to distract her, "Sharon, you hear that Robbie is back?"

"He is?" Sharon said. Sor stiffened his back and looked away.

"Yeah," Jason said. "Just before I left to come back here, da Vinci persuaded him to come back to the *Discovery*. That robot's the only one Robbie will listen to."

"That makes sense," Sharon said. "I don't think Robbie was too well treated by people in his own time. So he doesn't trust people. But da Vinci isn't a person. Robbie can feel different about him."

Jofrid smiled. "I believe you are right, Sharon."

Sor said coldly, "Maybe."

"Come on, Sor," Jason said. Put it behind you, man. Jofrid, we got to get back. Sharon, you need anything here?"

"No," Sharon said. The only thing she needed was to get Tara back.

When darkness fell, somebody brought Sharon and Sor pillows. In their s-suits, they were warm enough sleeping on the hillside. Sharon slept badly, with nightmares. How long could she go on like this? What were the Panurish doing inside their ship to her baby niece? Wouldn't anything about this nightmare ever *change*?

And then, the next morning, it suddenly did.

*   *   *

"Shar-on. Shar-on," said a hollow voice.

Sharon screamed, jerked awake, and screamed again. Standing on the hillside right in front of her, speaking *her name*, was a Panurish robot!

"Shar-on. Shar-on."

Sharon sat up. Sor moved quickly between her and the robot, but the machine didn't try to attack. Sharon stammered, "What? H-How . . . how do you know my name? Where's Tara?"

"Shar-on," was all the robot said. And it started back toward the ship.

Three paces, then it stopped. Turned. Came back to her.

"Shar-on. Shar-on."

Sor whispered, "I think it wants you to follow it!"

Sharon staggered to her feet. The robot started off again. Sharon said to Sor, "What should I do!"

Sor didn't answer. Sharon suddenly knew why. Following the robot could be incredibly dangerous, and Sor didn't want the responsibility for telling her to do it or not do it. But if following the robot might get Tara back . . .

Sharon squared her shoulders and let the squat metal creature lead her toward the Panurish ship. Sor stayed by her side.

Sixty feet from the ship, she felt a tingle go over her entire body. This must be the invisible electronic "fence" Jason had touched. A part of her mind wondered how tall the "fence" was. Could she jump over it with Tara?

No. The Panurish were smarter than that.

She walked toward the Panurish ship—but

Sor couldn't. The fence stopped him. "Sharon!" he called. "I can't get through!"

She didn't hesitate. "I have to get Tara, Sor!" She kept on walking.

The door to the alien ship opened, and Sharon Myers became the first human ever to walk inside a Panurish structure.

Immediately she saw Tara. The baby sat on a blanket on a floor of some strange blue metal. And something was definitely not right.

Sharon darted forward and grabbed Tara. Tara didn't even hug her back. The baby's eyes were glazed, and her little belly swollen. When Sharon grabbed her up into her arms, Tara suddenly vomited all over the blanket and the blue floor.

"What have you done to her!" Sharon screamed. "Tara! Tara!"

The baby clutched Sharon and started to wail, as if throwing up had actually helped bring her back to normal. And although Sharon hadn't expected any kind of answer to her question, the same robot that had brought her inside the ship spoke, in the same slow, hollow voice.

"Ta-ra eat. Ta-ra not good. Too bad, dude."

Too bad, dude? Suddenly Sharon realized what must have happened. The Panurish robots had overheard the human kids talking. From those conversations, they'd learned to speak English, at least a little. *Too bad, dude* was how Jason expressed sympathy or regret. The robots had picked it up from him.

Then the robot's actual words registered. "You fed Tara something that made her sick? What? Is she poisoned?"

No way to know if the robot understood all that. But maybe it did, because a flexible tentacle suddenly shot out of one of its sides. The tentacle held up a soft, bluish fruit the size of a tangerine.

Relief washed over Tara. It was one of the fruits that Sor had tested in his machine. It wasn't poison.

Sharon said to the robot, "That's not poison. Too much just gives her a stomachache, but—"

Abruptly, she stopped speaking.

If she told them Tara was okay, what would the Panurish do? There were no Panurish in this room, which was small and empty, but probably they were watching from somewhere. If Sharon told the aliens that Tara was fine now that she'd thrown up, what would they do? Probably just make Sharon leave and still keep Tara. No! That wasn't going to happen!

"Tara is very sick," Sharon told the robot. She made herself speak very slowly, in simple words. There was no way to know how much English the Panurish really knew. "Tara is very not good. I must help Tara. Do you understand?"

"Sharon help Tara," the robot said.

"And I must have medicine." Sharon seized on this idea wildly. Maybe she could even get more Yanks in here! That would increase their chances of winning any fight to get out.

"Medicine," the robot repeated. "Not a clue, dude."

"Medicine. Drugs. It means . . . it means special stuff that Tara eats to make her not sick!"

"Yes," the robot said. "Okay. Jofrid has drugs."

It knew who Jofrid was, and that she carried medicines in the pockets of her green dress! Sharon felt dazed. The Yanks had no idea that the Panurish and their robots had been watching humans so carefully. Watching, learning, probably running data through computer programs . . . and all this while, the humans had learned almost nothing about the Panurish. Too busy fighting among themselves or playing football!

Sharon tried to think. Jofrid wasn't the person she wanted inside this ship with her. Jofrid was small, not a fighter. She wanted Jason, or Sor.

"Yes, Jofrid has medicine," Sharon said. "But Jofrid cannot come inside your ship. Cannot." Why? Sharon thought wildly. "Jason is the leader. Only Jason can bring medicine near Panurish. Only the leader."

This time the robot was silent a long time. Was it thinking, or was it getting instructions from the hidden Panurish? There was no way to tell. Sharon held Tara tighter.

"Yes," the robot finally said in its weird hollow voice. "Jason is the leader. Tara is sick. Jason must bring medicine. There is a chain of command here."

That last, Sharon realized, was something Sor had once said. Sharon had overheard him. Apparently so had the Panurish.

The robot said, "Go tell Jason to bring medicine, Sharon. Leave Tara here."

"No!"

"Yes. Leave Tara here. Bring medicine. Bring

food Tara can eat. Go now. Bring Jason. Panurish are cool with that."

Sharon stood clutching Tara. "Okay," she said finally. "I bring Jason." She set Tara back down on the floor.

The door to the ship opened, and Sharon ran through it, calling, "Sor! Sor! Go get Jason—"

But Jason was already there. One of the kids on watch must have gone to get him as soon as Sharon was woken up by the Panurish robot. Jason stood just outside the sixty-foot defense zone, with what looked like three-quarters of the human kids clustered behind him, plus da Vinci. Sharon ran up to them. Once again she felt that strange tingle as she ran through the invisible "fence."

"Sharon!" Jason said. "What happened? Why did they take you inside?"

Sor cut in. "Where's Tara?"

"Inside," Sharon gasped, out of breath. "Safe. She just had a—" Suddenly she remembered that the Panurish were eavesdropping, learning English, putting everything she said into language banks, or whatever they were.

"Tara just had a bout of sickness. She needs some of Jofrid's medicine. Jason must bring it inside, because only the leader can carry items inside a Panurish ship, of course."

They all stared at her like she was nuts. Then da Vinci caught on. Sor must have reactivated him.

"Ah," da Vinci said, "of course. Jason must bring some medicine inside for Tara, since the Panurish know that our laws dictate that only a leader may do so. Jofrid, you must supply something that will duplicate the cure of Loki at Langerfoss."

Everyone looked baffled—except Jofrid. She broke into a wide smile. She must know what da Vinci was talking about, because she said, "I have the right medicine. But Tara must take it four times every day. And each time it must be made fresh. I will make it four times a day at the *Discovery*, and Jason will carry it in to Tara four times a day. If I do not, Tara will die!"

As Jofrid said this, she stared hard at Sharon, and gave a tiny—very tiny—shake of her head. Even in her upset state, Sharon understood. Tara was not in danger of dying. This was a trick to get Jason inside the Panurish ship as much as possible. The Panurish were aliens; they didn't know about human medicines.

Jason got it, too. He said loudly to Jofrid, "Go back to make the first batch of medicine, so Sharon and I can bring it inside."

Jofrid set off at a run. Sharon tried to walk back toward the Panurish ship. But a different alien robot—or maybe it was the same one— had followed her out, and now it stood just inside the sixty-foot defense zone.

"Wait, Shar-on," it said. "You go inside Panurish ship after you have medicine."

And there was nothing Sharon could do but wait for Jofrid to return.

Jofrid was quick. In twenty minutes she was back with a green powder carried in a metal cup from the *Discovery*. She handed it to Jason. He reached for Sharon's hand, and they started toward the ship.

The "fence" let them through. Sharon saw Jason give a small start of surprise and realized he must have felt the same tingling she did.

The door of the ship opened for them.

Inside was the same windowless, doorless, blue metal room, empty except for Tara. The Panurish were still hiding, and they'd made sure the humans couldn't get to them. But they—or a robot—had cleaned up Tara. She sat on a fresh blanket, dressed in her same clothes but now spotless, playing with her toes and gurgling happily. Never had Sharon seen a healthier baby. But maybe the Panurish wouldn't catch on to that.

Or maybe they would.

"Hey, Tara," Jason said. Then he spoke in the general direction of the bluest wall. "And hey, Panurish. How you doin'? I'm Jason, leader of the Jump expedition. I got medicine for this baby. Our doctor says I got to bring it fresh four times a day, so I'm going to be here. Maybe we can talk a little."

No response.

Jason handed the cup to Sharon. She didn't know what she was supposed to do with it, so she invented. She licked her finger to wet it, then rubbed it in the cup until every bit of green powder stuck to her finger. Then she put it in Tara's mouth. The baby tasted, grinned, and eagerly sucked Sharon's finger.

Sharon had a sudden suspicion that the green powder was nothing more than colored sugar.

"Now this baby will be all right until her next dose," Jason said loudly. "Everybody cool with that?"

No response.

Jason sat down on the floor. The robot said, "Jason leave now. Jason come with next medicine."

"No, I think I'll hang here a while," Jason said comfortably. "See who shows up, you know?"

The robot didn't answer. But suddenly Jason yelled, "Hey! That hurt!"

"What?" Sharon cried. "I didn't feel anything!"

"They shocked me," Jason said. "Just a little shock, but—" He stopped. He and Sharon looked at each other.

"Go, Jason," Sharon urged. "Go right away! They could fry you, the way they did Robbie. That shock was probably just a warning!"

"Well, maybe—"

"Go on! You're no good to us if you're dead!"

Jason nodded. He got to his feet. "I guess you're right."

The door to the ship opened. Jason walked through it, and instantly it closed.

Sharon and Tara and an alien robot were alone in a windowless, doorless blue room, probably watched by the Panurish.

This didn't seem to bother Tara at all. She'd gotten her socks off her feet and was happily chewing on one of them. But Sharon felt herself tense all over. What would happen now?

For a few long minutes, nothing did. Then the robot said, "Talk, Shar-on."

"T-talk? About what?"

"About anything. Talk human words."

Why? Sharon thought. Then she knew.

The Panurish wanted to learn as much human language as possible. What was it somebody had said last night? Enemies always tried to learn as much about each other as possible, to look for weaknesses. So anything Sharon said about human beings might be used against them by the Panurish.

Well, she wasn't going along with that! No way! Stubbornly Sharon closed her lips.

"Talk, Shar-on," the robot said.

Sharon said nothing.

Then she gasped. A painful electric shock ran over her left arm. It *hurt*. But only for a minute.

A warning, like Jason's. The Panurish were saying, *Do what we want—or else*.

All right, she'd have to talk. But nothing the aliens could use against human beings of this century! Sharon would see to that! They wanted words, they'd get words . . . but not Sharon's. And not new words. Old words, that would not give away any twenty-fourth-century weaknesses.

"This is 'Ode on a Grecian Urn,' by John Keats," she said.

" 'Thou still unravished bride of quietness,
Thou foster child of silence and slow
*   time . . . ' "*

Sharon was pretty sure she could remember the whole poem. If she forgot parts, she'd just make up nonsense words. How would the Panurish know the difference? And after the Keats poem, there were bits of other poetry they'd done in English class. Plus all the theorems from geometry. And the cheers for the Spencerville football team. And nursery rhymes! Let the

Panurish try to figure out human weaknesses from "Hickory Dickory Dock."

But first came the Keats poem about the lovely Grecian vase. Sharon groped for the words, reciting them clearly. Tara seemed to like it, too. She stopped chewing her sock and listened, smiling.

" 'Heard melodies are sweet, but those unheard
Are sweeter . . .' "

Still, reciting old-time information couldn't go on forever.

Jason better be out there thinking up a plan.

15

"**O**kay, everybody, big meeting just before dinner in the main chamber," Jason said when he and Jofrid returned to the *Discovery*. "I want every single last one of us there, ready to brainstorm."

Senta and Max, two of the *Discovery* kids, said they would tell everyone. In the meantime, Jason had another matter to take care of.

"Robbie," he said, "I want to talk to you in my room. Right now, okay?"

Robbie hesitated, nodded, and then followed Jason to his room. Jason closed the door. He sat on the edge of his bunk and motioned for Robbie to sit in the one chair.

Robbie stayed standing. He looked awful. One eye was black where Sor had punched him. His hair was matted and uncombed, and the clothes he wore over his s-suit looked even more ragged and dirty than when he'd come to Jump.

"First off," Jason said, "I want to say I got no hard feelings that you knifed me, Robbie. I know you were trying for Sor, not me, and that it was self-defense. We clear on that?"

Robbie nodded warily.

"What you did with Tara is a whole 'nother matter. But it's done now, and the thing we got to do is figure out a way to get her back. Right?"

Again Robbie nodded.

"So I want to start by you telling me everything—and I mean *everything*—about those pigbird fights you were running out there. Because there *was* a fight. I saw the dead pigbird myself, in that circle you drew. You already know how I feel about that. But what I want to know now is, who was at that pigbird fight?"

Robbie looked even warier than ever. Jason leaned forward. It made his bandaged side hurt, but he did it anyway.

"Look, Robbie, I know you weren't running a pigbird fight just so you could bet with yourself. You were running a fight to bet with somebody else and make some money. Or whatever kind of loot you hoped to get. Nobody on the *Discovery* would bet on two animals fighting to the death: they're way too kind for that. Sor hates violence, too, and so does Sharon. Jofrid can stand it, but she's not interested. *I* sure wasn't there. And I don't think da Vinci is programmed to bet on fighting. So who were you running that fight for?"

"Look, guv'nor—" Robbie said, and then stopped.

Jason said, "You had Panurish at that fight, didn't you? Betting on it."

Robbie looked at the door, back at Jason, at the door again. Finally he decided. "Yes, guv'nor. Panurish was there. But Robbie wasn't trying to hoodwink you, Jason! I was betting with them for the cube you been glimming your

160

daylights for! I was trying to win it from them!"

"And what happened?" Jason said.

Robbie hung his head. "My bird lost, guv'nor. Dipped badly, Robbie was."

"Robbie," Jason said, "do you think that even if you'd won the bet, the Panurish would have paid up with the communication cube? Do you really think that?"

Robbie looked more shocked than Jason thought possible. " 'Course they'd of paid, guv'nor! The one debt a man can't pike on is a gambling debt!"

Jason shook his head. Where Robbie came from, that might be true. Nineteenth-century London, Jason was beginning to realize, was almost as alien to him as the Panurish were. "Tell me everything, Robbie, from the beginning. Don't leave anything out. How did you get the Panurish to talk to you?"

"Didn't never talk," Robbie said. Finally he sat down in Jason's chair. "They found Robbie, they did. Few days ago, while they was out taking the air, marching along like they do. I caught two pigbirds to roast for dinner. Was going to roast 'em, guv'nor. Swear it on my eyes."

"And then . . ." Jason prompted.

"And then the Panurish come marching along and I thinks to myself, Maybe they're fighting men. Stands to reason they might be, guv'nor. Made that raid on the *Discovery*, they did. Took even her mainsails."

" 'Mainsails'? But the *Discovery* isn't. . . . never mind. So you set up a pigbird fight, and the Panurish stopped marching to watch it," Jason guessed.

"Right you are. And Robbie put a small wager on the ground, explained what *they* should wager back."

"Well, they probably understood you, since we know now they've been eavesdropping on everybody, learning English off us for free," Jason said. Suddenly he caught his breath. "Do you mean . . . Robbie, *did they put the communication cube on the ground to match your bet?*"

"Nah," Robbie said scornfully. "Not on the first bet. Start small, guv'nor, when you got a mark. I bet a small silver salt cellar I happened to have on me, and—"

"A what?" Jason said.

"A salt cellar. You know, for a gentry-mort's table, to hold salt. Real silver it was."

"Whatever. So you bet a salt shaker you stole five hundred years ago? What did the Panurish bet?"

"Couldn't tell you, guv'nor. Something small and strange-looking. But it was made of gold. Worth forking. Worth winning."

"Only you lost," Jason said. "Then what?"

"Then nothing. The Panurish go on marching away, and Robbie's left with catching another pigbird if I want a chance to get my own back again."

Only instead, Robbie had tried to trade Tara to the aliens. The betting hadn't worked to get the communications cube, so Robbie went on to the next idea. Which had also been a bust.

"Okay, Robbie," Jason said. "Now, I want to be sure I really understand. Tell me one more time. Everything that happened, from the top."

"Whatever you say, guv'nor." His sunny smile

was back. He was Robbie again: cheerful, confident, untrustworthy, unpredictable, dangerous to everybody else on Jump even when he was trying to help.

Jason sighed and concentrated on Robbie's story again.

Just when Jason thought things couldn't get any more stressed out, they suddenly did.

At Jason's meeting, fourteen kids and one robot sat in the main chamber of the *Discovery*, waiting for Jason to say something brilliant. The only ones missing were Corio and Wu, left on watch outside the Panurish ship, and Isor and Annit, on watch at the t-port site. Plus, of course, Sharon and Tara. Even Robbie was present, sitting in a corner far away from Sor. Robbie looked subdued. Maybe he really did regret losing Tara to the aliens. You could never really tell what Robbie thought.

"Okay," Jason said, because he had to start by saying something, "let's start by reviewing the situation we got here."

Nobody reacted.

"Well, first off," Jason said, "Tara's safe."

"However, the Panurish have her," da Vinci said.

"Second," Jason said, "Sharon is safe, too."

"However, the Panurish have her, too," da Vinci said.

"Third, the Panurish haven't found the communication cube, or they'd have left Jump already."

"However, we don't have the cube either."

Jason glared at da Vinci. Just what he

needed: a negative robot. "You know, da Vinci, you're a real downer."

"No, I am currently up, running on active."

"Right. Just keep quiet for a bit, okay?"

"Certainly," da Vinci said agreeably, and Jason turned back to the worried faces in front of him. "My point *is*, the game isn't over yet. We're barely past half-time. We can still get Sharon and Tara back, find the communication cube, get the t-port open, and all get back home."

Someone, Daryo, a quiet boy with large brown eyes, said, "How?"

"Well, we don't exactly have all the details worked out yet," Jason said, as cheerfully as he could. "We know that. But I'm positive that with all this brain power we got here, in just a little while—"

"Jason! Jason!" a new voice shouted, and Corio burst into the *Discovery*. Corio had been on watch at the Panurish ship. "Jason—they're leaving!"

"Who's leaving?" Jason said sharply.

"The Panurish! They've opened the t-port!"

Immediately everyone started talking, shouting questions at Corio, exclaiming aloud. "Quiet!" Jason yelled. "Everybody quiet! Let Corio make his report!"

People quieted. Corio stood panting in the main chamber of the *Discovery*; he'd run all the way from the Panurish ship.

"The Panurish have started to leave. They're carrying things to the t-port. They opened the t-port again! Wu and I followed them. I mean, they're not carrying stuff themselves—their robots are. All the stuff they stole from us!"

Sor said swiftly, "That means they haven't found the communication cube in all that stuff, and they're giving up. They're taking the whole pile home for their adults to sort through."

Jason frowned. "Then why didn't they do that in the first place?"

Deel said, "Maybe they didn't want to admit they couldn't find it alone."

"Yeah," Jason nodded, "makes sense. They wanted to complete the mission. Just like us."

Corio said, "They have seven robots carrying *our* stuff to the t-port, as much as the 'bots can carry. Then, during the ten minutes that the port was open, one kid went through with each robot and its load."

Jason said, "Did all the Panurish and all the robots come back to Jump?"

"Yes," Corio said.

Jofrid asked, "Did you see Sharon or Tara?"

Corio shook his head. "We waited until all the aliens went back to their ship, then we tried the t-port. But it didn't work.

Mikail said desperately, "Jason, what are we going to *do*? When the last Panurish leave Jump, they might leave the t-port jammed forever!"

Jofrid said, "They might also take Tara and Sharon with them."

That hadn't even occurred to Jason. Nor, from the looks on everyone else's face, to the other kids, either. Little Betta gasped and started to cry. Deel put his arms around the little girl.

Another girl, Tel, said, "Jason, you have to make a plan!"

Jason looked them all over slowly: it was his

responsibility to get them all home safely. Man, this didn't feel like being captain of a basketball team. This was real responsibility, big-time. And he didn't have his buds to help him, Clayton and Tyrone and Wayne. He didn't have big brother Brian to bail him out if he made a mess of the job. He didn't have Coach Patterson to blame if the play didn't work.

He only had himself.

"Okay," Jason said. "I have a plan. But it's gonna take all of us here to carry it out. Especially you, Robbie. Everybody—listen up real good."

16

By afternoon of the next day, Sharon was completely hoarse. She was also more scared than she'd ever been before in her life.

All yesterday, plus all today, she'd been talking to the Panurish robot. Her throat hurt from talking. The one time she'd stopped, the Panurish had hit her with another electric shock. So she kept on talking, and by now she was running out of things to say.

She'd tried to stick to her resolve not to say anything that might give away valuable information about contemporary humans. So she'd recited a mishmash of things: Old poetry. Geometry theorems. The Gettysburg Address. Nursery rhymes. Lyrics to old songs: "Happy Birthday" and "Yellow Rose of Texas" and "Yankee Doodle." Grocery lists. Characters in old TV shows. Let the Panurish robot try to gain military information from the names of the Brady Bunch!

The only breaks came when Jason was allowed in with more "medicine" for Tara. Each time, she hoped Jason would do something to get them out of there. But it hadn't happened.

Jason had been allowed to give Sharon some food and the cup of colored sugar, and then he was pushed back out the door. The last time, however, he'd whispered softly to her, "Get outside."

"Wait," Sharon finally said to the robot. "Stop. Don't shock me, either, please. Look at Tara—she's full of energy. You have to let us outside for a while, so she can crawl around. You know we can't get through that electronic fence!"

"Okay, Sharon," the robot answered. "We'll take our speech lessons outside."

Fear hit Sharon. The robot was talking English so much better than it had before! Was that because of the things she'd been reciting? Could a computer program really improve its sentences by listening to "Yankee Doodle" and "Three Blind Mice"?

Evidently it could.

The door to the ship opened. Sharon picked up a squirming Tara and carried her outside. After twenty-four hours in the tiny blue-metal room, she blinked at the bright afternoon sunlight. And then she blinked at something else.

The pile of equipment from the *Discovery* had diminished by at least half.

Had the Panurish given the stuff back to the human colony? No, that didn't make any sense. The Panurish must have carried it off somewhere, or, rather, had their robots do it, since the aliens themselves were so small and weak. But where? The only place that made sense was the t-port. The Panurish must be planning on taking all the equipment off Jump.

Would they take her and Tara, too? And then what?

"Talk, Sharon," the robot said, and despite her fear, she did. There wasn't any choice. She put Tara down about ten feet away from the ship, on the soft groundcover. The baby crowed and began to crawl around happily. Sharon talked.

"Once upon a time there were three pigs. They each built a house, one of straw, one of wood, and one of bricks . . ."

As Sharon talked, her voice hoarser every second, things began to happen around her.

First, eight Panurish and seven robots emerged from the ship. The robots picked up more of the *Discovery* equipment and balanced it on their smooth flat surfaces. When the seventh robot had finished, there was no stolen equipment left on the ground.

"Where are they going?" Sharon asked the eighth robot, the same one that had been guarding her and listening to her and filling her with fear. "Where are they taking all that equipment?"

"Talk, Sharon," the robot said.

Sharon talked. The Panurish marched over the top of a hill and out of sight. It seemed to Sharon that they moved faster than they had on their previous marching expeditions. It almost looked like the aliens were excited about something.

"Talk, Sharon," the robot said. "Don't stop talking."

"My throat is so dry!"

"Drink some water. Then talk."

Half an hour later Sharon was in the middle of a plot from *The Simpsons*. Tara had fallen asleep in her lap. From the direction of the *Discovery*, a crowd of kids walked toward the Panurish ship.

They stopped about twenty feet outside the "electronic fence." Sharon could see them clearly. Mant, Billin, Betta, Deel, Sor, Cam, Jofrid, Annit, Mikail, Isor . . . everybody but Jason, Robbie, and da Vinci. Odd.

What they did next was even odder. They began to play *football*.

"Talk, Sharon," the robot said. "Don't stop talking."

Yes, it *was* football! Was Jason completely crazy? Here she and Tara were prisoners, the Panurish were preparing to t-port off Jump, nobody had found the communication cube, and Jason's idea of a plan was to organize a game of *football*?

She watched, incredulous, as Sor organized two teams. Sor, who was usually so sensible and compassionate! He didn't even glance at Sharon, and neither did any of the others. Yet she knew they could see her clearly. In an effort to get as far away from the Panurish ship as possible, she and the robot sat near the electronic barrier.

"Sixteen, forty-two, eight, hike!" shouted Mant, and snapped the ball to Cam, who started to run with it. People ran after her. Jofrid fell and stayed down, doing something in the groundcover. Deel caught Cam. Another play started. The ball they were using for this game was really large and, judging from the way it flew through the air, heavier than usual. The outside was made of blanket, tightly wrapped. At the far end of the makeshift field, Sharon saw, were extra balls, in case this one got wrecked.

"Ten, three, hike!" Betta cried in her thin high little-girl voice. She threw the ball. She was a lousy thrower: the ball hit the invisible fence about six feet above the ground and was immediately fried. The game stopped while Deel fetched another ball from the supply.

"Talk more, Sharon," the Panurish robot said. "Say more words."

Sharon was half-way through the plot of *Titanic* when Billin also threw a bad pass. This one was higher, however, since Billin was older and stronger than Betta. The ball sailed through the air about eight feet above ground and went over the top of the "fence." The robot beside Sharon fried it.

"Out of bounds!" someone cried. "Get another ball, Alli!"

The game resumed. Then Sharon saw Jason walking toward the Panurish ship through the running mass of football players, carrying the metal cup with "medicine" for Tara.

Nothing unexpected about that—it was time for one of Jason's four-times-daily visits. But Jason looked subtly different. Sharon tried to see why. Jason walked like a person who was very excited about something but trying not to show it.

The robot listening to her saw Jason and called to him, "Come in." Jason walked through the invisible fence and over to Sharon.

"Hi, Sharon."

"Hi," she said, grateful for the chance to stop talking.

"Hi, Tara, baby doll."

Sharon's eyes widened—Jason was talking to Tara? Voluntarily? Calling her "baby doll"? What on earth was going on?

Jason said, "I brought your medicine, Tara-doll. Come over to Uncle Jason and get it."

Sharon almost fell over. Tara, who was possibly the world's friendliest baby—this world's, certainly—crawled over to Jason's outstretched hands and let him pick her up. He held her as if he'd never held a baby before, which he probably hadn't. Then Jason spoke to the robot.

"How you doin', metal guy?"

"Talk, Jason," the robot said. "Say words."

"Say what?"

Sharon whispered—her voice was nearly gone by now—"It wants you to tell it stories. It's recording us, I think, to learn more English."

"I don't know—"

"Tell it anything!" Sharon said desperately. "I'm all talked out. Tell it about football! Or basketball!"

"Okay," Jason said, and actually patted Tara on her back. "I'll tell it about the last game I played at Franklin High. You see, we were behind three points, and then Wayne does a three-sixty and . . ."

Jason talked on and on, the robot facing him instead of Sharon. Could the Panurish learn anything to use against Earth from Jason's description of something called a "full-court press"?

". . . and then Tyrone dribbles and shoots, and then he . . . Now!"

And then everything happened so fast that Sharon could barely follow it.

Jason kicked the Panurish robot as hard as he could. At the same time he sprinted toward the electronic fence, only a few feet away from where they'd been sitting. The robot fell over but almost immediately righted itself and swiveled around to fry something.

Jason had reached the fence. In a blur he crouched, pushed off with his feet, leapt high in the air. And threw Tara.

"No!" Sharon heard somebody scream, and realized it was her. Tara would be killed, fried when she hit the fence, just like the stray footballs . . .

But she wasn't. Jason, so tall and so fit, had jumped in the lighter gravity high enough to dunk Tara over the top of the electronic fence. And there was Sor underneath, ready to catch her in a sort of blanket, while Jason screened them both with his body. Then Jason would be fried! But he wasn't because he was standing absolutely still inside the fence, and the Panurish robots only fried things that were moving.

The robot darted forward, through the suddenly-open gate, and started to chase Sor, who was running with Tara wrapped in a blanket. But then the robot stopped. *Everybody* was running—or at least five or six people were. They all carried blankets the same size as Tara, and they ran by each other and passed the blanket-wrapped bundles back and forth. The bundles were extra footballs, the very big footballs . . . The robot didn't know now which one held Tara. It couldn't tell! Except . . .

"It won't work!" Sharon screamed. She remembered what da Vinci had told her: the Panurish robots could detect body heat. And that's what it was doing now, scanning each bundle in turn, swiveling its sensors towards one after the other . . . Only it didn't move. Why not?

Finally the robot did move, so fast that it was even more of a blur than Jason had been. It took off after Deel, who was running like the wind toward the *Discovery*. Sharon felt Jason grab her hand. "Run, Sharon! It left the gate open!"

She ran, crying, "The robot will fry Tara!"

"No, it won't. Run!"

Jason pulled her along. They ran after the robot, with no hope of catching up. But the robot easily caught Deel, since Deel, carrying Tara, had suddenly stopped. Fear froze Sharon's heart. Why would Deel stop! Now the robot would kill them both—

The robot tripped.

It went down very hard, and the next minute Deel, too, had dropped to the ground with Tara. Sharon ran, her heart bursting. Some of the others reached the robot first. They were doing something to it, throwing something on it . . . Sharon couldn't see. She ran past them, to where Deel lay panting on the ground.

"Tara! Tara! Is she hurt?" Sharon cried.

And Tara poked her head from under the blanket, laughing and laughing.

The baby thought the whole thing was one big game!

"Run, Sharon," Jason urged, "back to the *Dis-*

covery. But stay very very low, like this. Go!"

Sharon grabbed Tara and ran, crouched over. Tara was heavy, but Sharon clutched her like she might never let go. At the *Discovery* she ran inside, followed by all the others, who had caught up with her. Deel closed the doors and everyone collapsed onto the floor of the main chamber, breathless.

When she could speak, Sharon gasped, "How . . . how did you do that? What *happened*?"

Everyone tried to talk at once. Jason held up his hand, and gradually everybody quieted. Jason said, "We planned it all. Dunk the baby over the fence, once we found out from frying extra footballs exactly how tall the fence was. Then a multiple fake-out so the Panurish robot wouldn't know who had Tara. It scanned with its body-heat sensors, but . . . but . . ." Jason ran out of breath.

Betta took up the story. "But all the blankets showed body heat!" she crowed, "Because they had pigbirds wrapped in them! Pigbirds that Robbie caught!"

"And *then*," Mant said, "the stupid robot had to spend time doing detailed scans, not just heat-sensor, to see which one was Tara. By that time Deel had run with Tara to Jofrid's snares—"

"They were set in the groundcover, by a pit!" Billin cried.

"Let me tell!" Mant yelled. "The snares tripped the robot and pulled it into the pit. And we threw brush on it to cover its motion and light sensors, and *lots* of dirt—"

"—and that gave us all time to get back here safe!" Deel finished.

Sharon felt dazed. So much planning! Basketball, football, pigbirds, snares, pits . . . and it had all worked. Everyone was safe inside the ship, except—

"Where's Robbie?" Sharon suddenly asked. "And da Vinci?"

"Everybody fell silent. After a minute Jason said, "They're safe, too. We hope."

"But where are they?" Sharon persisted.

Jason said, "All the Panurish went this time to the t-port to send stuff through while it's open. Usually one or two stay behind, as you know, but we needed them all to go. So you'd be left with just the robot to guard you. So Robbie's been running a gambling thing, with da Vinci's help, by the t-port. It turns out the Panurish like gambling. They all went."

Sharon said, bewildered, "A 'gambling thing'? What kind of gambling thing?" A horrible thought occurred to her. "You don't mean . . . Jason, you're not letting him make pigbirds fight to the death just to distract the Panurish!"

"No, no," Deel said. "Robbie promised he wouldn't hurt any animals in his gambling game. Whatever it is."

And you believed Robbie? Sharon wanted to say. But she didn't. A second, even more horrible thought had occurred to her.

"Jason—there are eight Panurish by the t-port. And seven of their robots. When the robot in the pit gets loose and goes to tell them you rescued Tara and me, won't the Panurish get really mad? What if they take it out on Robbie and da Vinci?"

Nobody answered. Then Jason said quietly, "Yeah, you're right. And we all thought of that. But Robbie insisted on taking the risk. He said it was to make up for losing Tara to the Panurish in the first place. Frankly, I didn't know he had it in him."

"Neither did I," Sor said quietly. "I misjudged him."

"A brave dude," Jason said. "And good at getting out of trouble. My bet is he'll be back hanging with us in no time."

Sharon hoped so. Jason had said Robbie was good at getting out of trouble. But it didn't seem that way to Sharon. It seemed to her that Robbie was mostly good at getting into it.

17

"**H**ere they come," da Vinci said. "Remember, they have never attacked anything or anybody that didn't look like it was attacking first. Just don't make any threatening moves."

"Nobody got to tell Robbie how to handle a mark, metal guv'nor," Robbie said. "Robbie's worked Whitechapel, Covent Garden, Bartholomew Fair."

"Those words are not in my data banks, but I presume they are place names in which you have succeeded in swindling people. But you have never swindled any Panurish before."

"People, Panurish, all the same to Robbie," he said cheerfully. "The Panurish coves are fresh marks, metal guv'nor. Plain as pikestaffs."

Da Vinci and Robbie stood beside the t-port, which was of course still jammed. It was late afternoon. In front of Robbie was a metal table carried from the *Discovery*. On it rested a collection of objects, some brought from the ship and some fished out from the inner pockets of Robbie's dirty coat.

A line of Panurish approached: eight of them, marching along in strict formation, accompanied by seven robots. Each robot carried another load of equipment stolen from the *Discovery*. Aliens and robots marched up to the t-port and stopped.

The eight aliens looked directly at Robbie, standing behind his table.

"Got 'em," Robbie said softly under his breath.

Da Vinci began to recite the speech Robbie had taught him, with a few additions of his own. "Step right up, ladies and gentlemen and artificial intelligences, for the most exciting gambling games you ever glimmed your daylights on! Far superior to betting on pigbird fights, far superior to faro or rouge-et-noir, far superior to outrunning a supernova shock wave! Far superior to anything you've ever experienced! Test your skill! Test your luck! Test the laws of probabilities! Win prizes what nobody could expect to own in your life!"

The Panurish didn't change expression. Or maybe they did and neither Robbie nor da Vinci could tell, because the expressions were so alien. But the Panurish all—every one—took one step away from their robots and one step closer to the table.

"That's right, then!" Robbie said. He picked up a deck of cards he'd brought with him from nineteenth-century England and started to flash them around. One-handed shuffles, dazzling snaps. He threw them in the air, where they all fanned out, and then somehow he caught the cards neatly, in one smooth pile, and snapped them loudly. He smiled.

The Panurish all took another step closer to the table.

"Good, good, alien guv'nors," Robbie said. "Now watch this."

Deftly he took three cards from the deck: the two of hearts, the two of clubs, and the queen of diamonds. He laid them, face up, in a row on the table and pointed to them. Then he turned up the middle one and said, very slowly and clearly, "The Queen!" Next he turned all three cards over, face down, and quickly slid them around the table top. Faster, faster . . . until he stopped and the three cards were again in a row, face down.

"Now, Master da Vinci," Robbie said, "which one be Her Majesty the Queen?"

Da Vinci pretended to hesitate. Finally he picked one of the cards. Robbie turned it over. It was the two of clubs.

"You lose, Master da Vinci!" Robbie crowed. "Good thing for you we wasn't betting that time! Care to make a small wager now? Here's Robbie's bet."

Slowly, so the Panurish would be sure to understand, Robbie took an object out of his pocket. It was his best knife, the small thin deadly one with which he'd wounded Jason. All the Panurish took another step closer to the table.

Robbie said, "What's your bet, Master da Vinci?"

Da Vinci pretended to think for a moment. Then he reached toward his own belly. A door opened in him, a door that hadn't been there a moment ago, and he removed a flat thin sheet of smooth metal and laid it on the table.

The first Panurish in the line let out a long

low musical note that anyone in the universe would have recognized as surprise.

Robbie said, "That's your wager, then, Master da Vinci? Fine by Robbie."

Once more Robbie held up the queen of diamonds to let everyone see which one it was. He replaced it on the table, face down with the other two, and began to slide the three cards around. Faster, faster . . . until he stopped.

"Where be Her Majesty the Queen, Master?"

Da Vinci hesitated, thought, finally chose. He picked the queen.

"You won!" Robbie said, pretending to look upset. He pushed both his knife and da Vinci's data chip toward the robot, who picked them both up off the table. "Try again, guv'nor? Here's a prize!"

From the pile of objects at one side of the table, Robbie pulled out a vase made of metal with painted interrupted lines forming a design over the metal. It was the vase Sharon had found amid the debris of the *Discovery*, the vase that had reminded her of English class back home. Robbie pushed the vase toward da Vinci. The robot nodded and put his computer chip next to the vase.

The Panurish ignored the vase, which they could have stolen from the *Discovery* on their first raid if they had wanted to possess it. Obviously they didn't. But seven of them eyed the computer chip steadily. The eighth glanced at Robbie's knife, dangling from da Vinci's tentacle.

Robbie and da Vinci played the card shuffle again. Faster, faster . . . da Vinci won again.

Now he had the computer chip, the knife, and the vase.

One of the Panurish kids said something to the others.

It was the first time any Panurish had ever spoken in front of a human. Its voice was high, squeaky, and weirdly musical, almost like bad violin playing. Another Panurish answered. Then it looked like an argument, everybody squeaking at once. Abruptly it stopped, and one Panurish stepped toward the table.

The Panurish pointed with its short, skinny arm toward the cards. Next it pointed toward the knife that da Vinci held. Then it reached into one of its own pockets and pulled out a hunk of metal and laid it on the table.

The hunk of metal didn't look like anything humans made. It was about six inches long, shaped like a lumpy sweet potato, silver on one end and red on the other. Da Vinci pretended to study it, and then nodded. He put Robbie's knife on the table beside the thing.

"Bets all placed?" Robbie said. "Then here we go!"

He showed the queen to da Vinci and the Panurish, placed it face down with the other two cards, and slid them around the table. Faster, faster, faster . . .

The Panurish won.

The alien gave a high, sharp squeak and grabbed up both Robbie's knife and his own lumpy whatever-it-was. A different Panurish crowded him out of the front row and pointed to the cards. Then all the aliens, their long silence forgotten, were squeaking and producing objects and pointing to what they wanted to gamble for.

Robbie grinned at da Vinci.

Half an hour later, the Panurish had won a lot of items: Robbie's knife, toys from the *Discovery*, a bracelet of carbon-alloy gems, an antique watch with a picture of King George III on it, a silver flask ... But somehow, they couldn't seem to win the computer chip. All the Panurish watched while da Vinci opened his belly once more and put it back inside.

The sun touched the horizon.

The Panurish started chattering to each other. One spoke to their robots, who all this time had been waiting patiently, loaded with stolen equipment. Now the first robot in line lumbered forward and waited in front of the place the t-port had once shimmered.

The sun went down.

Robbie and da Vinci both watched very carefully. Robbie didn't see any of the robots make a movement. But just at sunset, the t-port shimmered open again. And da Vinci gave a tiny nod of his metal head toward the fifth robot in line, making sure that Robbie saw the nod.

That was the Panurish robot that gave the invisible signal, whatever it was, to jam and unjam the t-port. A different robot put in a load, a Panurish stepped in with it, and the whole thing vanished. A minute later the Panurish kid reappeared. He rushed back to the gaming table. A different Panurish kid accompanied the next load, then rushed back.

"All right, ladies and gentlemen!" Robbie said

loudly. "One more chance to win! Them what is badly dipped can get their own back again, and them what is winning can do even better! The biggest game of the day! Anybody want to make a wager? Here be mine!"

And Robbie pointed to da Vinci.

"That's right, Metal Masters Panurishes! Robbie's wagering this here metal man, for one of yours. On a single turn of the card. Who's sporting cove enough to take the bet? You? You?"

The Panurish all broke into violent squeaking. They shoved up against one another, waving their furry arms. Clearly they disagreed about betting one of their robots against da Vinci. So far they had paid up all their bets, although Robbie didn't believe that they'd let him keep a Panurish robot. It might finally force them to cheat on the bet. Why not? *He* was cheating. He kept an extra card in his sleeve so he could make the game come out any way he wanted. He was so fast with his hand movements that no eyes, human or Panurish, could detect his substitutions. Sometimes he let the Panurish win, sometimes he prevented their winning. It was all part of his and da Vinci's plan.

By now, Jason should have gotten Sharon, Tara, and all the other human kids back into the *Discovery*.

The third Panurish robot loaded its stolen equipment into the t-port. It waited. Finally, with obvious reluctance, a Panurish kid tore himself away from the argument and jumped into the t-port to accompany the load of stuff. As soon as he could, he rushed back to the table. The fourth robot unloaded its equipment into the t-port.

"Wager or not?" Robbie said. "I bet da Vinci against one of yours?"

More squeaking. No Panurish kid got into the t-port with the fourth robot. Clearly they didn't want to miss any of the gambling. Finally the Panurish leader turned around and squeaked something at the robot in the t-port. It vanished with its load . . . and without any Panurish kid accompanying it.

The Panurish leader pushed forward one of its own robots to stand next to da Vinci, and gestured toward the cards.

Robbie showed the queen. He placed her back on the table, face down, and slid the cards around. Faster and faster . . .

The fourth Panurish robot reappeared and stepped out of the t-port. The fifth robot, the one that controlled the t-port's jamming and unjamming, stepped in with its load.

Faster and faster and faster . . . "Choose!" Robbie cried. "Where be Her Majesty the Queen?"

The Panurish leader seized one of the cards and turned it over. It was the two of clubs.

All the Panurish started yelling in shrill, ear-splitting squeaks. The robot that Robbie supposedly had won moved away from him. The fifth robot and its load of stolen goods disappeared through the t-port. And da Vinci, moving suddenly at blinding speed, picked up the heavy metal gaming table and threw it at the t-port.

Immediately the nearest Panurish robot sent

out a beam that fried da Vinci. He crumpled into powder right there on the purple groundcover.

Robbie stood very still, making no threatening moves, making no moves of any kind at all.

The table da Vinci had thrown had landed half in and half out of the t-port. The t-port shimmered as if it were trying to bring back the fifth robot, stopped shimmering because the table was there, shimmered again, stopped. It looked like a broken Christmas-tree light, blinking feebly, unable to come fully on while the huge table was in the way.

The Panurish squeaked frantically. A different robot rushed forward to pull the table out of the way. The moment it touched the table, however, *the robot* fried and crumpled into powder.

The Panurish acted panicked. They ran around in circles, squeaking. Then they all ran back toward their own ship, followed by their robots.

In five minutes they were out of sight over the closest of the low hills, and Robbie was alone.

Very slowly he walked toward the t-port. He waited. In a few more minutes, the shimmer disappeared. The t-port was closed until the next evening.

Next he went over to the pile of powder and small, twisted metal fragments that had been da Vinci. Robbie spoke to the powder.

"You was right, metal guv'nor. They can't fry nothing what sits in that magic door, even partway in. And you was right about the big thing, too. Those Panurishes was cowards. 'Any man who panics is halfway lost already,' you said, and you had the right of it. Robbie admits you had the right of it."

It was dark now, except for two of the smallest moons. The air was growing colder. Robbie sat down on the grass next to what was left of da Vinci.

"Robbie hopes, metal guv'nor, that you was right about the rest of it, too. You said you ain't dead. Sure looks dead to Robbie, you do. But I got your soul safe, just like you told me." And from his pocket he drew out the computer chip that had originally been in da Vinci's belly.

To Robbie it didn't look like much: just a flat bit of metal. Not even sharp enough to cut anything. You couldn't get two shillings for it in London. But the metal man had said his soul was on it. Robbie didn't see how that could be. But maybe it was so. Maybe the other coves would know, them what came from this place. That gentry-mort Sor, or Deel, or even Jason, what was supposed to be the master here. Best to wait and see.

He put the microchip inside the painted vase. Then, in the growing darkness, beside his shattered robot friend, Robbie sat and waited for Jason and the others.

18

Cautiously Jason opened the main door of the *Discovery* just a crack. He peered out. No Panurish, no Panurish robots. Of course, they could be hiding, just waiting for humans to emerge before they fried them. Next, Jason stuck his arm out the door. Nothing happened. Then he stuck his head out, followed by the rest of his body.

"Be careful," Billin said behind him. Yeah, right. Like there was any way to do this carefully.

Jason squeezed his body through the crack in the door and stood outside.

It was a lovely night, warmer than any so far on Jump. The lemony smell was stronger, too. Only two moons were up, but they were both full. When Jason's eyes had fully adjusted, he could see pretty well. He moved away from the ship. Nothing fried him.

"Okay, come on," he said. Billin, Sor, and Annit slipped out after him. He nodded and the four started toward the t-port site. Sor held his laserlight but didn't turn it on.

Let Robbie be okay, Jason thought as his long

legs hurried along. Just let that thieving little twerp be okay, whether or not da Vinci had accomplished anything about the t-port. Robbie had already succeeded in his main mission: he'd kept all eight Panurish occupied and distracted long enough for the Yanks and the *Discovery* kids to steal Tara back. *Just let Robbie be okay*.

"Come on!" Billin said in a loud whisper. "Run!"

"Billin, wait!" Jason said sharply. "I go first!" If something had happened to Robbie, something awful, Jason wanted to see it before Billin did. Billin was only ten. If whatever awaited them at the t-port was too gruesome, Jason would order the boy back to the ship.

But the scene at the t-port wasn't gruesome, because there was no scene at all. No Robbie, no da Vinci. Only a table half-in, half-out of where the t-port had been. It looked weird: one part of the metal table lying on the ground, looking normal if upended, and the other part connected to it but looking sort of shimmery, outlined, like it wasn't really *here* but it wasn't really *there* either. A ghost half-table.

"What the—" Jason said. The four looked at each other.

Slowly they walked closer. Billin, who had the best hearing, said suddenly, "What was that?"

"I didn't hear anything," Annit said.

Jason shivered. The empty darkness, the table stuck halfway into the t-port. . . .

"Listen again!" Billin cried, and this time Jason heard it, too. A voice sounding like it was trying to both whisper and shout at the same time.

"Are—you—ghosts?"

"Robbie!" Jason cried joyfully. "You're here! No, we're not ghosts, it's really us! Come out!"

"Show—Robbie—you're—not—spirits!"

"He's scared," Annit said. Her voice was compassionate. "In his time of history, everybody believed in ghosts and spirits. He thinks the Panurish might have killed us all."

"Well, all right, I'm cool with that," Jason said. "Only how do we prove to him we're not ghosts?"

"I don't know," Deel said. "Sor?"

"I don't know."

The four non-ghosts stared at each other. Then Billin called, "Robbie! Watch this!"

He jumped as high as he could, as if he were making a jump shot, and whacked Jason on his left shoulder coming down.

"Ow!" Jason cried.

"See?" Billin called. "He's solid! And ghosts don't play basketball either!"

"Couldn't you find some other way to convince him?" Jason demanded, rubbing his shoulder. But apparently it worked. After a minute they could make out Robbie coming toward them from his hiding place in a clump of bushes. He walked warily, holding something in one hand, and as soon as Jason could see his face in the moonlight, Jason knew something was wrong.

Annit said, "Robbie, where's da Vinci?"

"Dead," Robbie said.

Dead? How could a robot be dead, Jason wondered. Sor could just turn him back on. Unless . . .

Robbie said, "The Panurish, they fried the

metal guv'nor. A knowing one, he was. May his soul rest in peace."

"Amen," Jason said, without thinking. But then Robbie added, "Only Robbie got his soul here. Metal guv'nor said so. How can that be, Sor?"

It was the first time since their fight that Robbie had ever addressed Sor directly. But that wasn't as astonishing as Sor's response. His handsome face lit up and he said, "Let's see!"

"See a soul?" Jason blurted out, because the whole thing was getting too weird. Both Robbie and Sor ignored him. Robbie raised the thing in his hand, which Jason now saw was a vase from the *Discovery*, and turned it upside down. A flat metal rectangle fell out, and Sor whooped with joy.

"You got it! You got the identity chip!"

And then Sor—*Sor*, who as far as Jason knew hated Robbie's guts—picked up the small thief and danced around with him. And Robbie—*Robbie*, who as far as Jason knew had tried to kill Sor—let himself be picked up and danced around with.

"Okay, okay, stop," he said. "Sor, put him down. Robbie, you make your report. Everything, from the top."

Annit said, "Shouldn't we go back to the ship? For safety?"

"Never should do it," Robbie said. "The Panurish, they might come back, and then we'd be all to pieces. We got to guard the table."

"The *table*?" Jason said, wondering if whatever had happened to Robbie had scrambled his brain. "Why would we guard a table?"

"No, don't touch it!" Robbie screamed at Billin, who had curiously approached the table. "It'll fry you, it will!"

Billin jumped backward. Jason looked from him to the table, to Robbie, and back to the table. Why didn't he ever know what was going on?

"Okay, Robbie," he said, "we'll guard the table and nobody'll touch it. But right now everybody else shut up, and *you make your report*. Annit and Sor, you stand guard, one facing east and the other west, but close enough to listen. Everybody cool with that?"

Everybody was. Robbie licked his lips a few times. He was obviously still shaken by whatever had happened. Jason was suddenly very curious to know what could shake Robbie.

"We start, metal guv'nor and Robbie," he said, "by dragging this here table from the *Discovery*. For the swindle. We put the cards on it. But before that, before Panurish even flock to the deep doings, metal guv'nor does something to the table. Fixes it up right and proper, he does, for later. 'But you can touch it now, Robbie,' he says. 'Just run your gambling games.'

"And I do. The Panurish, they think they're up to all the tricks, but they ain't. They never seen the extra cards in Robbie's sleeve. I gammon 'em all, and let them win when I want, and make them lose when I want. 'Cause what they want is this *thing* here. Soon's they see it, they want it."

"Of course they do," Sor says. "It's the main identity and library chip for one of our most advanced robots. You heard da Vinci say how much simpler their 'bots are than ours. They'd learn a lot more about us from that than from listening to Sharon talk. Or from any of the electronics they stole from us, because those are all at least six years obsolete."

Jason said, "If they wanted the chip so bad, why didn't they just take it? There were eight of them, plus seven robots, and just two of you."

"Can't do that, guv'nor," Robbie said, looking shocked. "Vowels can't be whiddled! Any other kind o' debt, yes, nothing in that, but not vowels!"

Sor said dryly, "He means that the Panurish will steal anything they can get their hands on, but they never welsh on gambling debts. Da Vinci explained it to me. The Panurish culture, like Robbie's, apparently bets heavily, and honesty in paying gambling debts is what holds the culture together. Otherwise it would just collapse into everybody fighting everybody else. It's bred into the Panurish not to cheat at games of chance, and they programmed their 'bots to be like themselves."

"Saw it for meself at the first pigbird fight," Robbie said, but this topic made Sor look upset, so he dropped it. "Them metalmen, they still owe me a robot I won from 'em. They'll pay it, come time. But meanwhile, *our* metal guv'nor, he rigged the gaming table. Then he bet his soul—"

Robbie held up the identity chip "—and I knew never to lose it. I just tantalized 'em with it, like. Finally them Panurish wanted it so bad they was drooling. So we made 'em a last grand bet. I bet metal guv'nor."

"You bet *da Vinci*!?" Billin said. "But he's a sentient AI!"

"Metal guv'nor told Robbie to bet him," Robbie said unhappily. "Like he told Robbie about the Panurish metalmen. Watch, he said. We need to know which one puts the shining magic door in the basket."

"What?" Jason said.

Sor translated again. "I think he means that one of the robots sent the signal that jammed and unjammed the t-port machinery, and da Vinci figured out by electronic scanning which one it was. So then what, Robbie?"

The small kid looked tired. He said, "Robbie bet metal guv'nor, and Robbie won. We timed it to an inch, we did. The Panurish metalman took his load through the shining door, and vanished, he did. Metal guv'nor grabbed the table and threw it, he did, into the shining door. And a Panurish robot fried him. Just like he said they would. He knew, metal guv'nor did, what the lay would be. Panurish panic—they're cow-hearted, every last one of 'em!"

Listening, Jason had a sudden insight. Robbie was upset big-time because of da Vinci's death. Robbie clutched the vase with da Vinci's identity chip inside as if he'd never let go. The ragged runty thief had loved da Vinci. Jason hadn't thought Robbie could love anybody.

"Go on, Robbie," Sor said gently.

"Panurish run around squealing like the pigs they be. One o' their metalmen grabs the table to pull it out o' the shining door. But metal guv'nor rigged it. The throw did it. The table crashes into something, and the table turns dangerous."

"Impact-activated weapon system," Sor said. "So when one of the Panurish robots tried to pull the table out of the t-port, the table fried it?"

"Right you are," Robbie said. "Then everybody panics more. Squealing and running, all the way back to their ship. But metal guv'nor's still dead."

Jason drew a breath. He couldn't get over how brave this skinny uneducated little thief was. Robbie didn't understand any of what da Vinci had arranged: not the t-port unjamming or the impact-activated lasers or even that they all stood on another planet. Robbie thought it was all spirits and ghosts and magic doors. Yet Robbie had still saved them all. Jason felt enormous respect.

Sor said gently, "But Robbie, da Vinci isn't really dead."

"Saw him fried with me own daylights!" Robbie cried.

"Yes, I know. But you have his essential identity in that vase. It can be installed in another robot body."

Robbie shook his head. Clearly he thought Sor was crazy. In his world, dead was dead—at least for people, and to Robbie, da Vinci had been a person, not a machine.

And I think so, too, Jason thought. Da Vinci had been a lot more like a person than like a machine. Jason hoped Sor was right, and the computer nerds of 2336 could recreate da Vinci. But right now, there were more pressing matters.

"Robbie, are you sure that da Vinci said the t-port is unjammed? Why can't we see it?" Jason asked.

Sor said, "It will be working normally as soon as we remove the table. Normal working means it only comes on for ten minutes at sunset, remember? Until then, the Panurish can't open the t-port no matter how much energy they try to expend, because it's jammed on this side. It's a safeguard built into the system so nobody t-ports into a port that already has an object in it. Your molecules would get all mixed up with theirs."

That didn't sound good. Jason tried to think it through. "Okay, so right at sunset we pull the table out . . . Whoa, how are we going to do that? *We'll* get fried!"

"I don't know," Sor admitted.

"Annit? Billin?"

They shook their heads. Finally Jason said, "Okay, we got about twenty-two hours to figure that out. Let's say we get the table out. Then the t-port is open and everybody goes through it. Only don't we end up at Panurish? That's where the aliens were going when they took our stuff through it."

"No," Sor said. "I can fix that. Remember when Dr. Cee and da Vinci both told you that this sort of limited-time t-port is different from most t-ports? It's only open a short time every day, and *also* it's flexible. It responds to the co-ordinator field on the first person through. I have the switching device on me."

"You sure? You haven't lost it? Check now," Jason said nervously. All this time on Jump, and he never realized that getting back depended on some little gizmo in Sor's pocket.

Sor smiled. "I know I haven't lost it. It's sewn under my skin."

"Eeeuuueewwww," Jason said. But he was relieved. "Next problem: How do we keep the Panurish from coming back tomorrow night, after they stop being scared, and frying us all before we t-port home?"

Nobody had any ideas.

Jason said, "So that's two problems. We got to get this wired table out of the t-port, and got to keep the Panurish scared inside their ships."

"Plus," Billin said helpfully, "we still have to find the communication cube. Don't forget that, Jason."

Jason sighed. He had forgotten. He'd been so caught up in getting Tara back and everybody home alive. But the communication cube was still the point of the mission, and they didn't have it yet.

"Thanks a lot, Billin," he said sarcastically.

"You're welcome, Jason," Billin said politely. 2336, Jason remembered, didn't understand sarcasm.

"Okay," Jason said. "Back to the ship. We need input from everybody if we're going to figure out what to do next."

At the *Discovery*, everybody wanted to talk at once. Finally Jason stood on a table—his life seemed to be full of tables lately—and yelled at everybody to shut up. "One at a time! Let's start at the beginning. Okay, what do we know so far? Sor?"

Sor said, "Well, one thing we know for sure is that the Panurish all panicked when da Vinci threw the table, and then they panicked even more when it fried a Panurish robot."

"Yeah," Jason said, "you're right. They did. What else do we know about the aliens?"

Mant said, "They think it's very important to pay gambling debts."

"Well . . . yeah. But we did the gambling thing once already. What else?"

Cam said thoughtfully. "They made Sharon talk and talk, to learn everything about us they could. And they wanted da Vinci's identity chip for the same reason."

"Good," Jason said.

Billin said. "They're cowards. They don't ever go anywhere alone, and they need their robots to protect them, and they run away when anything strange happens."

"Yes!" Jason shouted. "That's it!"

"What's it?" Sharon said, confused.

Jason said, "All of what people just said. Something strange happened—something the Panurish didn't expect because it wasn't in their data banks—when da Vinci wired the table to be a weapon. And that unexpected thing made the aliens fall apart. So what if we go to the ship and do all sorts of things the aliens don't expect? Confuse them big-time? That will make them want to stay safe inside, watching, until they think they got a handle on us. Only we don't let them *get* a handle."

Sor frowned. "How do we do that?"

"We behave all different from whatever we usually do," Jason said. Everybody stared at him. They didn't seem to be getting it. Jason sighed and tried again. "Okay, Billin, what do you usually do?"

"Do?"

"You know, *do*. When you're just hanging with people."

Billin thought. "I talk to them. I play football with them. I help gather plants to eat. I run around. I—"

"Okay, that's enough. Tomorrow when we're at the Panurish ship, you're going to do the opposite of all that. You're going to make nonsense sounds, not real talk that the Panurish have already learned. You're going to bury a football instead of throwing it. You're going to gather plants you know we can't eat and then cook them. You're going to crawl instead of run. Whatever we all usually do, we're going to do something else. The Panurish won't have a clue what's going on—and they'll want to know, because they're like that. They'll stay inside, observing, having their robots process all this weird data, instead of going back to the t-port, because they're cowards."

Everyone began to talk at once, arguing about the plan, thinking up things to do that would confuse the Panurish. Finally Wu said, "It won't work indefinitely."

Jason said, "It doesn't have to. All we have to do is keep the Panurish away until sunset tomorrow. Then we can leave Jump through the t-port ourselves."

Annit tried to say something, but Mant outshouted her. "But the table's still blocking the t-port! We'll get fried if we try to pull it off!"

Jason said, "Jofrid has a plan for that. She talked to me about it earlier. Jofrid, take the people you need for your plan—but not too many, 'cause I need most everybody to act weird at the Panurish ship. Take . . ." Jason thought rapidly. "Take Sharon, Robbie, Mant, Betta, and Wu. Is that enough?"

"Yes," Jofrid said.

"Then you better get started. Everybody else, we won't start acting weird till morning, but we're going to the Panurish camp right now. Let's go."

As they walked to the t-port site, Sharon carrying the sleeping Tara, Jofrid said to her, "Jason is smart."

"Why do you say that?" Sharon said. She hadn't been outside on Jump at night very often. Because of Tara, she hadn't been standing watches like the others. The planet was lovely at night. Moons dotting the sky, luminous stars, a light warm breeze smelling of lemons and pine. If only the Panurish weren't here, Jump would be a wonderful place to live.

Jofrid said, "Jason's smart because of who he picked to come with me. You, because you don't want to take Tara back anywhere near the Panurish. Robbie, for the same reason. Betta, because she's the youngest and should be protected from danger. Wu because he's so strong. Mant because he is so cheerful, and we will need that as much as Wu's strength."

"We will?" Sharon said. "Why?"

"Because digging tires both body and temper."

"Digging? What are we going to dig?"

"Wait," Jofrid said, "until I tell everybody at once."

When they reached the t-port, she did. Jofrid, so short, stood on a little mound of earth and addressed her troops.

"Where I live, in Iceland, there are no trees. Wood is very precious. We save it for things like rafters, the High Seat, and the women's cross bench."

Her four listeners stared uncomprehendingly. Sharon knew what the others were thinking: What's a High Seat? Or a women's cross bench? And what does this have to do with the deadly table blocking the t-port?

Jofrid continued, unperturbed. "Because we have no wood, we must build with turf. We cut blocks of earth to make our houses and cowsheds. We move the blocks by rolling them on logs, round like these." She held up two long cylinders of metal. Sharon recognized them: They were legs off a table on the *Discovery*.

"We will dig," Jofrid said. "First we will dig a deep trench in front of the table-that-burns, so deep and so well-placed that the table topples forward and falls into the trench. Then we will roll blocks of earth on top of it until it is buried. Then we will construct walls of earth around the t-port, so that if the Panurish robots come, their fire bolts will hit earth and not us."

Mant cried, "The ground doesn't get fried when Panurish weapons fire at it! It scorches but it doesn't disappear!"

"So Jason noticed when we threw dirt over the robot chasing us with Tara," Jofrid said, smiling. "After it fell in the pit and we covered it with dirt, it couldn't destroy anything. We will do the same with the table-that-destroys."

We said, "An effective plan."

Little Betta said, "Let's get started!"

"In the morning," Jofrid said, "when we can see what we're doing."

Wu said, "Tonight we're just here to guard the t-port. Get as much sleep as you can, everybody. We're going to need our strength tomorrow."

Yes, Sharon thought. Just like Jason and his group was going to need their ingenuity. Could they really act weird enough, long enough, to keep the cautious Panurish inside their ship, safe and observing—and away from the t-port?

They'd find out tomorrow.

Everyone settled down to sleep. Sharon put Tara between her and Jofrid, well wrapped in blankets from the *Discovery*. Everybody else had their s-suits. The last thing Sharon noticed before she drifted off was Robbie. He lay curled into a ball around the vase that held da Vinci's identity chip, protecting it with his scrawny body from the darkness and cold.

19

The next morning, the sun rose on two groups of humans already hard at work.

"Be careful, Mant!" Sharon said worriedly. "Don't get too close to the table—it's dangerous!"

"I won't," Mant said. "This is fun, isn't it?"

Sharon just looked at him. It wasn't *her* idea of fun. She, Wu, and Mant stood in the ditch they'd been digging since first light. The ditch started a respectful foot in front of the deadly table blocking the t-port. Already the ditch was three feet deep and a foot longer than the table looming above it. The diggers used shovels brought from the *Discovery*. This was difficult for Sharon because the shovels were designed for 2336 adults, who must have been really *tall*. Sharon's neck, shoulders, and back hurt, and she was covered in dirt. She felt hot, achy, and sweaty.

Jofrid came to the edge of the ditch. "Is it our turn yet?" She, Robbie, and Betta were the second shift of diggers. Robbie had insisted on digging despite his burned hand, which Jofrid had wrapped in layers and layers of cloth.

"Your turn soon," Wu said. "Mant, if you get any closer to that table, I'll fry you myself."

Mant laughed. "Isn't this *fun*?"

Grimly, Sharon lifted another shovelful of dirt.

"Wimney kisty willy boo!" Sor shouted.

"Fizzle frokin googoo pox," Billin answered. He crawled toward Sor, leaped straight up in the air, screamed, and sat down calmly, smiling.

Jason watched them from a few feet away, where he was trying to grow leaves. He stood very straight, like a large tree, holding branches from a bush in either hand. More branches were tied to his ears. Every once in a while he waved the branches gently, as if ruffled by a breeze.

What did the Panurish make of all this? There was no way to tell. The aliens and their robots stayed shut up tightly inside their ship, behind their electronic barrier. Just outside it, fourteen human kids did everything weird and unexpected that they could think of. Were the Panurish robots taking this all in? Trying to fit it into the language banks? Sorting the behaviors to find reasonable patterns? Trying to understand those patterns before the Panurish risked coming out again?

Good luck!

"Shibble shibble johnson's hat!" Jason suddenly shouted, and started to eat his own branches.

"Watch it, Robbie, careful—get out of the way! Get out of the way!" Jofrid yelled.

Robbie leapt nimbly out of the ditch, which

was now very deep. It angled inward, under the table. A second later the table started to slide. Slowly it slid forward, breaking off more dirt as it moved. Gathering speed, it toppled into the ditch in a spray of dirt. The ghostly shimmer across half of it disappeared—now it looked like a regular table resting in a regular ditch.

"Yeah!" Mant yelled.

"Don't go near it yet!" Jofrid ordered.

After a minute, the table had settled fully into its hole. Cautiously Jofrid threw a shovelful of dirt on top of it. A small rock was fried instantly, but most of the dirt settled over the table. Wu threw in a second shovelful.

"Not that way, do it like this," Jofrid said. "It's easier on the back."

Wu threw another shovelful just as Jofrid had showed him. So did Robbie.

Ten minutes later, the table was buried. Wu and Mant grinned at each other. Tara, watching from a safe distance, gurgled happily. Betta clapped her hands. Robbie said softly into the vase, which was never far from his side, "See, metal guv'nor's soul? We done it, we did!"

And Jofrid suddenly stopped in her tracks and looked dazed.

"What is it, Jofrid?" Sharon asked worriedly. "Isn't everything going the way it's supposed to?"

"Yes, fine," Jofrid said, still looking surprised. "It isn't that. I just—" She stopped.

"You just what?"

"I just . . . realized. I'm giving orders to men. Me."

"So?" Sharon said.

"In Iceland, women don't order men. Ever. But here, I am telling Wu and Robbie what to do, and they're doing it."

"Well, it's *your* plan," Sharon pointed out.

"Yes. But Wu and Robbie don't seem to dislike me for speaking my mind."

"Of course they don't," Sharon said warmly. "Everybody likes you."

Jofrid stood thinking a minute longer, frowned, shook her head, and suddenly smiled. It was the most open, full, sunny smile Sharon had ever seen from her. But all she said aloud was, "It's very strange."

Annit crouched over the football. "Seventeen, fourteen, St. Petersburg, hike!" Then she sat down on the ball.

Everyone applauded wildly. "Your point!" Jason yelled. "Minus three!"

The Panurish ship remained shut and silent. The sun stood directly overhead. It was already noon.

Wu and Sharon strained to lift a large block of earth onto the other blocks, which were equally large. The dirt cube was much heavier than it looked, Sharon thought—who knew dirt weighed so much? With a final grunt, they got it wedged in place.

"Good!" Mant cried. "It looks great!"

Stepping back to look at the earthen wall, Sharon had to agree. Four blocks high and four long, it was a solid barrier as tall as Jason. Another wall just like it was set at a right angle, giving them two sides of a dirt shed around the t-port. It looked good.

What didn't look good was all of the builders. Sharon had never been so filthy in her entire life. She could feel dirt in her hair, in her boots, even in her teeth. Jofrid's wool dress had so much dirt on it that you couldn't tell what color it was underneath. Mant looked like a mole.

"Now we build the third wall," Jofrid said.

"Oh, Jofrid, can't we rest first?" Wu asked.

"Well, yes, perhaps. For a few minutes."

They all sat down next to the wall, admiring it. Tara lay asleep in the afternoon sunshine. Jofrid said, "At home, we would have a skald recite a saga now, or a poem. Sharon, can you recite a poem?"

Sharon felt dog-tired, not in the mood to recite anything. Talking so much for the Panurish robot had made her want to just sit silently. But Jofrid was her friend, so she said, "Okay. What poem?"

"Any poem. The one about the Grecian vase."

"Okay.

'Thou still unravished bride of quietness,
Thou foster child of silence and slow
*   time . . . '"*

As she recited, Sharon watched Robbie. This was a good poem to recite for him, since it was about a vase and Robbie continued to cling to the vase with da Vinci's identity chip in it. Not that Robbie made the connection, of course. He wasn't even listening to her. Neither were Billin or Betta. Sharon was reciting for Jofrid, and herself, and maybe for the always-quiet Wu.

" 'Beauty is truth, truth beauty—' "

Saying the beautiful old lines, watching Robbie hold the vase, something tugged at Sharon's mind. She couldn't quite get it. The poem, the vase, talking and talking and talking to the Panurish . . .

"Thank you, Sharon," Jofrid said. "Now, everybody back to work. We still have two more walls to build before sunset."

"Here's the thing," Jason said solemnly to the four kids sitting on the ground before him, just outside the Panurish electronic fence. "Humans can get superpowers by linking their minds."

Billin raised his hand. "So why don't we do that now?"

"Oh, I know!" Cam called. "Let me answer, Jason!"

"Okay, Cam, you answer."

She said, "The reason we can't link minds now and get superpowers is that it only works for adults and it only works in a vacuum."

"That's right," Corio said. "Our warriors can only do it when they're in space, outside the ships."

"But when they do it, they gain enough power to blow away anything up to a mass of forty million kilograms," Mikail said.

Cam said proudly, "My uncle Danno is a mind-link warrior. With the Black Brigade."

Jason looked at them with admiration. What

liars they were! This was some of the best bull he'd ever heard. And it sure made humans sound mad, bad, and mean.

He hoped the Panurish were listening hard.

"Three walls," Sharon whispered. She couldn't talk loud; her throat felt too full of dirt and dust.

"No time for a fourth wall," Wu whispered, in the same condition.

The three dirt walls cast long shadows across the purple groundcover. Half an hour, Sharon estimated, until sunset. No one had come near them all day, neither Panurish nor humans.

Wu whispered to Jofrid, "Stop now?"

Jofrid nodded. All of them sat down on the ground to watch the horizon, waiting to see who would come over it. They were too tired to talk. They just sat, waiting, Robbie clutching the vase with da Vinci's identity chip.

Robbie. The vase. The poem . . . The thing that Sharon had been trying to remember before teased again at her mind. What was it? Something about the vase, the poem, talking to the Panurish . . . Once again, she couldn't quite bring her thought into focus.

But then another thought did spring into focus. No matter who came over the horizon, these were her last minutes on Jump. The last minutes for all of them.

If Sor appeared and changed the t-port setting, they were all going to march through it and go home. Sor back to 2336. The *Discovery* kids, too, who hadn't been home in seven years. Jofrid would go back to Iceland in 987, Robbie to London in 1810, Jason to New York City. And she,

Sharon, would go back with Tara to Spencerville and never see any of the others again.

A sudden sadness swept over her. Jofrid was
the first real friend she'd ever had. Sharon
would miss her.

"Someone's coming," Mant said suddenly. He
had the best hearing. "Over the hill."

All at once Sharon's heart began a slow,
hard pounding in her chest. She could hardly
breathe. "Get into the hut!" Jofrid said.

The six humans scrambled behind the
earthen walls. It would only buy them a few
minutes, but a few minutes seemed infinitely
precious. If the Panurish were coming—

"It's Jason!" cried the irrepressible Mant. "It's
Jason and everybody!"

The human kids strode over the horizon,
walking briskly and close together, a purposeful
team. Sharon felt dizzy with relief. Now if only
the t-port shimmered into place the way Sor
said it would!

"Okay, we're here," Jason said, as fourteen
kids rounded the corners of the three-sided
earthen hut. "Look at you all! You look like
you're made of mud!"

"You don't look so great yourself," Mant retorted. "Why are there leaves tied to your ears?"

"Never mind that," Jason said. "Jofrid, you
got the table out and buried, good job!"

Even through all the dirt on her face, Jofrid
glowed with pleasure.

"Okay, listen up, everybody," Jason said.
"Final-play time. When that t-port shimmers
on, we're out of here. I don't think those chicken
Panurish are coming after us, but we don't know

for sure. So Sor first, to set the coordinates of the t-port to Edge Station. Then the youngest kids: Betta, Mant and Billin, then Sharon with Tara. Then everybody else. I go last, with Sor and Deel and Annit. If we—"

"Jason," Deel said. "I can't go."

"Say what?" Jason said. Then Sharon saw him stop and look at Deel, really look at him. Deel's face was sad but determined.

"I can't go," he repeated. "Neither can Annit or Cam. And probably Mikail shouldn't try it either. I thought you understood. We're too old."

Jason gaped at Deel.

"We're not really kids anymore," Deel continued bravely. "Annit and I are nineteen. Cam is seventeen, and Mikail is sixteen and a half. If we try to t-port now, what happened to our parents could happen to us. Adults can't t-port."

"You mean . . . you mean you're stuck on Jump?" Jason blurted.

Annit lifted her chin. "I prefer to say that now Jump has become our home."

For a moment, no one spoke. Sharon felt intense admiration. Deel, Annit, Cam, and Mikail seemed to her the bravest kids she'd ever known.

Sor said suddenly, "But you needn't be alone in your home. Now that we know that the colony is alive, people from 2336 can set coordinates for this t-port. They'll send supplies and tools. And kids can come visit you. *I* can come visit you!"

Jofrid said, "And have you young kin in Sor's city? He can tell them where you are, and they too can visit."

Mikail said excitedly, "I had a cousin!"

"Me, too," said Cam. "A whole family of cous-ins!"

"Good, good," Jason said. "But look—we got no more time, team. Here comes the t-port!"

Sharon jerked her head around to look. Within the three-sided earthen hut, where a moment ago had been only emptiness, a rectangle shimmered.

"Here come the Panurish!" Billin shouted, looking back at the hill.

"Go, Sor!" Jason yelled. "T-port!"

Sor jumped into the shimmer and vanished. Swiftly Jason pushed Betta in after him. Billin followed her. Sharon took one frantic peek around the edge of the dirt hut. Eight Panurish kids and seven Panurish robots stood on the top of the nearest hill. But they were standing, not coming forward. Were they too cautious to come down to the t-port until they understood what this new dirt hut was and what had happened to the table that had fried one of their robots? Oh, let the Panurish be that cautious long enough for everybody to get out!

"Deel, Annit, Cam, Mikail—run!" Jason shouted. "Go back to the *Discovery*—the aliens won't follow you. They're too busy with us. Bil-lin, Mant—go!"

The four oldest colony kids took off at a wild run, circling around the Panurish to get to the *Discovery*.

"Sharon—go!"

Jason grabbed Sharon, who stood holding Tara, and shoved them both through the t-port. Sharon felt a faint tingle, and then someone else was grabbing her, pulling her free of the precious portal. It was Dr. Cee, and Sharon was back in 2336.

The room was full of people. They kept pouring in through doors on either end of the t-port chamber: not just Dr. Cee and Dr. Orgel but also a lot of other people Sharon didn't recognize. Then, through the t-port, Corio appeared. Everybody was shouting. Tara started screaming in Sharon's arms.

"Jofrid!" Sharon shouted, adding to the general noise. "Get Jofrid out!"

Ali tumbled through the t-port booth, and was snatched out of the way to make room for the next kid.

Next Wu.

Then Isor.

Billin screamed, at everybody and nobody, "Are they attacking yet? Are the Panurish frying anybody?"

Senta.

Max.

"Where's Jofrid?" Sharon cried. "Is she fried?" More people crowded into the room from hallways, all talking. "Where's Jofrid?"

Daryo.

Tel.

Finally Jofrid shimmered into shape in the t-port booth. Sharon tried to push her way toward her. She couldn't; there were too many people in the way. Sharon got stuck between two adults, and could only watch as Jofrid was yanked out of the way. Somewhere behind her she heard Mant say to somebody, "No, we didn't find it. We didn't get the communication cube."

Robbie shimmered into shape in the t-port

booth. He clutched the vase holding da Vinci's identity chip. And at that moment, it all came together in Sharon's mind. All at once, she *knew*.

The vase. The poem. Da Vinci. Talking to the Panurish.

"I said we don't have the communication cube!" Mant yelled more loudly, evidently trying to be heard.

"Oh, yes, we do," Sharon whispered, but no one heard her over the noise.

Jason shimmered into view, the last human kid through. He blinked to see so many people, so many strangers, crowded into their home-coming, all talking and shouting questions and hugging *Discovery* kids. Jason held up a hand, but before the room could quiet, the t-port shim-mered again.

Even though everybody was through!

A flash of metal, and a Panurish robot ap-peared. Billin started screaming, "It's going to fry us!" and the room exploded into frenzied fear. Kids rushed for the doors. But then some-how, over all the incredible noise, Robbie made his voice heard.

"The Panurish pay off their vowels, they do! Robbie was owed a alien metalman, and here it be!"

"It's payment on a debt?" Jason screamed, and Robbie nodded happily and put his hand on his new property.

Slowly the room calmed down. Sor said, "Now we can learn as much about the Panurish as they know about us, after all!"

"Dr. Cee," Jason said, "can we—"

But before he could finish his sentence, Sharon heard another voice: a voice louder and more assured even than Jason's. After a shocked moment, she realized the voice was her own.

"Jason, *I know where the communication cube is.*"

And all the noise started over again.

20

"**A**ll right, Sharon, just say whatever you want at your own pace," Dr. Cee said. She smiled kindly at Sharon, who still felt a little shaky. Too much tension, too little food. She hadn't fainted, exactly, but right after she spoke up in front of everyone—she, Sharon, who had once been too afraid to open her mouth in class!—she had started trembling. Dr. Cee and Dr. Orgel had cleared the room of most of the shouting people. The scientists who worked here were gone, and so were the Jump kids, who'd been taken someplace to phone their aunts and uncles. Or however you contacted long-lost relatives in 2336.

The Yanks had insisted on staying. So Jason, Sor, Jofrid, Robbie, Sharon, Dr. Cee, and Dr. Orgel sat around a conference table. The adults looked crisp and clean in their white clothes. Sharon, Jofrid, and Robbie were covered in dirt. Sor didn't look too bad, but why did Jason have leaves tied to his ears?

She *was* feeling shaky. She tried to concentrate on what was important here.

"About the communication cube," Dr. Cee said.

"That's just it," Sharon said. "There *is* no communication cube."

"Come again?" Jason said, at the same moment that Sor said, "But, Sharon, in the cube that Captain Kenara made after the Gift Givers landed the *Discovery*, he said that he recorded Step Three in a second cube—"

"No," Sharon said. "Captain Kenara said he recorded Step Three. He didn't say it was in a cube. We just all assumed it was in a cube because that's how his dying speech was recorded. And maybe because cubes are the usual way of storing information in this time—aren't they?"

Dr. Cee nodded. "Yes."

Sharon said, "But there are other ways of storing information. That's why the Panurish took everything electronic from the *Discovery*, right? Because they didn't know just how Captain Kenara would code his information. It might be in any kind of computer program. But computer programs aren't the only way to code information, either."

Sharon took a deep breath. "I put it together because I remembered the Panurish making me talk and talk so they could learn all about humans, to defeat us. I tried to give them stuff that was so old it wouldn't reveal anything about humans today. I recited an old Keats poem, 'Ode on a Grecian Urn.' That made me think of da Vinci's identity chip that Robbie keeps in that vase, even though he doesn't really understand what an identity chip is."

Robbie scowled. "Metal guv'nor's soul, Sor said. He did."

"Yes," Sharon said. "Robbie thinks about computer chips in . . . in the words of his time. He doesn't understand computer language. Just like I didn't understand the language of semaphore, that the cheerleaders in Spencerville were using in their Technology & Communications project. Not until I looked up the meanings of their flags, in the encyclopedia. It was in a language nobody uses any more."

"Sharon, dear, I think you must be very tired," Dr. Cee said gently. "You're not making sense."

"Yes, I am," Sharon said. "Don't you see?"

"No, babe, not yet," Jason said. "Keep talking."

"The *vase*," Sharon said. She reached across the table and took the vase from Robbie's hand. "Captain Kenara wanted to put the Gift Givers' information in a form that no enemy aliens could read. So he didn't use a communication cube. He did what Keats did—he saw in a vase a way of teaching lessons. And he did what *I* did, reached back in time for something old so that the Panurish wouldn't know what it was. I wouldn't have even known what it was if it weren't for my research for my school project."

Sharon held up the vase. In the soft light of the room its curved metal shone. Beautiful sleek lines, and the decorations painted on the bottom, colorful interrupted lines, some long and some short.

"The Gift Givers' information is right here," Sharon said, touching the vase's painted decorations. "All you need to know about the next step for human beings. It's all here." She ran her hand again over the dots and dashes that Captain Kenara had hastily painted on as he lay dying. Dot-dash, space, dot-dot-dot.

"It's right here," Sharon said. "In Morse code."

The next morning the Yanks had a long meeting with the Edge Station scientists. "Debriefing," Jason called it, and he seemed to love it. So did some of the others. Sharon didn't, not really; she'd have preferred to just talk quietly with Dr. Cee and Jofrid. Although she liked sitting in the big conference room, the same one she'd seen when she first came to Edge Station, with the walls that kept shifting color. Violet to blue to blue-green to green. It looked so beautiful.

Actually, *everything* looked better after a bath and shampoo and a long night's sleep. Five Yanks and eleven Jump kids sat around the huge table, clean and excited and eager to tell their adventures.

Sor and Jason told about the way they kept the Panurish confused that last day on Jump. Jofrid told about trapping and burying the deadly table in a pit. Billin and Mant, as irrepressible as ever, told about the basketball-football game to rescue Tara from the Panurish.

Only Robbie refused to relate his story of gambling to keep the Panurish occupied during Tara's rescue. The small street thief looked better when he'd had a bath and his eighteenth-century clothes were washed, but he didn't look any happier. His was the only unsmiling face around the big table. Dr. Cee had taken the vase

219

so the computers could read the Morse code, but Robbie kept the identity chip that had been inside it. He refused to let it out of his fist.

"It's metal guv'nor's soul," he kept saying.

Finally Dr. Cee asked Jofrid and Sharon to persuade Robbie to give it up. Doubtfully, they said they'd try. They got Robbie alone in the corridor outside the conference room.

"For just a little while, Robbie," Jofrid said. "Give da Vinci's soul to Dr. Cee for just a little while. She promises you'll see it again. Don't you trust her?"

"Don't trust nobody," Robbie said.

"But this afternoon we're going to take a tour of this city. You can leave your treasure here for that long, can't you?"

"No," Robbie said.

Suddenly Sharon had an idea. "Robbie—what did you call those things that a person has to pay, no matter what? The gambling debts?"

"Vowels," Robbie said. "Man got to redeem his vowels."

"Yes. Suppose Dr. Cee gives you a . . . a 'vowel' for da Vinci's soul? Then would you let her have it for a while? You know Dr. Cee would redeem a vowel."

"Have to," Robbie said. "Well . . . all right. Robbie will take the doctor's vowel."

Dr. Cee, when Sharon and Jofrid told her about this conversation, said, "Good work! Only . . . what does a vowel look like? Never mind, I'll ask the library computer."

Evidently she did, because she presented Robbie with a handwritten piece of paper.

"There, Robbie—a vowel for da Vinci's identity chip."

Robbie looked suspiciously at the paper. Then he handed it to Sharon. "Read it for Robbie, then?"

Sharon nodded. She hadn't realized Robbie couldn't read.

Owed to Robert of London: one identity chip for the robot da Vinci. To be repaid by this evening, unless Robert of London should choose to forgive the debt. Interest due, to be paid at same time: ten pounds.

Robbie said, "Robbie don't forgive no debt."

"You don't have to forgive it if you don't want to," Sharon said. "The vowel just says you *can*."

Robbie nodded. He pocketed the paper in his baggy brown pants. He didn't smile.

"Be of good cheer, Robbie," Jofrid said. "Tonight is the feast. Even on Jump they will feast—right now people are preparing to take a celebration to Deel and Annit and Cam and Mikhail. And all the other *Discovery* children will leave tomorrow morning for the homesteads of their kin, so we must enjoy our last celebration together. Dr. Orgel will announce the meaning of the Morse runes on the vase."

Sharon said anxiously, "You'll come to the celebration, won't you, Robbie?"

"Robbie be there." But he still wasn't smiling.

That afternoon, the five Yanks got a special tour of 2336.

"All you've seen of the future so far is the inside of this one building," Dr. Cee said. "Edge Station One isn't London or Mars City or Titania, of course, but at least it will give you the flavor of the future."

The flavor of the future, Sharon thought, was *dazzling*.

The Yanks followed Dr. Cee through the door—and immediately clutched each other for support. The ground was distorted. No, not distorted—just strange. In two directions it stretched away normally, with streets and buildings and a little park. But in the other two directions, left and right, the ground curved away so quickly that Sharon couldn't see the bases of buildings less than a hundred feet away. It was as if the horizon was pushed up close to her . . . but only in two directions, not four. And the tops of the buildings leaned away from her, like pictures she'd seen of the Leaning Tower of Pisa.

"Weird," Jason said. "I think we ain't in Kansas anymore, Toto."

Dr. Cee smiled. "Let me explain a bit about Edge Station. What the Gift Givers presented to humanity was a main sally port, which was a huge object shaped like a tin can."

"A what?" Jofrid said. Of course, Sharon thought: There were no tin cans in medieval Iceland. Dr. Cee tried again. From her pocket she took a folded piece of metal. When she unfolded it, it turned into a rigid computer screen, thin and flat.

"On—draw a cylinder," Dr. Cee said to the computer, and the computer did.

"Magic," Jofrid breathed.

"Make sure nobody don't fork that thing," Robbie said.

"Does Bill Gates know about this?" Jason said.

"Go on," Sharon said. "You said the Gift Givers presented humanity with a cylinder. Where is it now?"

"You're standing on it," Dr. Cee said. "The cylinder is two miles long and a third of a mile in diameter. Inside is the alien technology that drives both sally ports and t-ports. It's a rotating gravity-line vortex which includes an exponential fall-off of the gravity field as you leave the center, of an e-folding length of three hundred meters."

Jason said, "Physics is senior year, and I'm not there yet."

"I'm sorry," Dr. Cee said. "You don't want to know the details. Let me just say that the Gift Givers made the first cylinder, and humans built a second cylinder around it. On—draw a second cylinder encasing the first. See, we built our city between these two cylinders. That's where you are now."

"You mean that's not sky up there?" Jason said. "It's a humongous tin can instead? Sure looks like sky."

"We light it to look like Earth," Sor said. Sharon realized he must know all this already. It made her feel a bit strange. On Jump, Sor had been just another one of the Yanks. Now she remembered that he was at home in this strange culture so far ahead of hers.

"Look at those flowers!" Jofrid suddenly said. "Oh, what are they?"

The Yanks had walked behind Dr. Cee into the little park. Now they stopped in front of a flowerbed of pink-and-purple blooms, each one as wide as Sharon's hand. But it wasn't just their size that made them so striking. Each flower was perfect, and the designs on the petals of each were different. A wonderful, spicy fragrance floated on the air.

Dr. Cee said, "They're genemod—genetically modified. We can change flowers' DNA to create any species we want."

"Magic," Jofrid repeated.

Sharon looked around her—really looked. It did seem like magic. She had never seen any place so beautiful. The buildings clean and graceful, glowing with faint color. The lovely little park, without litter or broken bottles or smashed benches. But it wasn't the environment that Sharon noticed now. It was the people.

Three little kids, playing happily in a sandbox, watched by a robot just as da Vinci had watched Tara on Jump.

Two adults walking past, deep in conversation, looking as if the subject fascinated them both.

Three more adults having lunch at a sort of outdoor café on a little platform surrounded by miniature waterfalls and more genemod flowers. The people laughed and nodded at each other.

Jason said suddenly, "Where are your homeless?"

Dr. Cee said, "We don't have homeless, Jason."

Sharon said, "You mean, you don't have them here, on this space station. But on Earth you do."

"No," Dr. Cee said. "We don't."

"You bamming us," Robbie said. His eyes had narrowed to slits.

"No," Dr. Cee said. "Let's sit down. There's something I want to explain to you all."

They went further into the park and sat down on a group of benches. More children played just beyond. The view of buildings and houses from here was just as wonderful.

"This is why I wanted you to see the future," Dr. Cee said. "*Your* future. I know there is a lot of misery in each of your times. Homelessness, poverty, disease, starvation, drought, war. And Sharon and Jason, it's only going to get worse in the century after the one you left. The Times of Trouble are coming. I won't go into detail, but I will say that humanity goes into a crisis, or rather a series of crises, so bad that it will look doubtful for a long time whether people will survive on the planet at all."

Dr. Cee's voice became intense. She leaned forward on her bench toward them, as if trying to will them to understand something of immense importance.

"But, Sharon, Jason—*humanity did survive*. We came through, partly because of the sacrifice and intelligence and sheer grit of a group of human beings scattered all over the world. They kept civilization going, and slowly *homo sapiens* pulled out of the Time of Troubles. And when it was over, we began the slow process of learning how to eliminate all mankind's old enemies:

Violence. Desperation. Disease. Poverty. Hunger."

"You did all that?" Jason said. "You mean, like, it's heaven here now?"

"No," Sor said. "People still get into private disappointments and all that. But society as a whole works now, for the first time ever, for every single child born into it."

Sharon tried to think what that would have been like for her. A life that worked. Her mother not a drunk, her father still around. Johnna taking care of her own baby, responsible and stable. Robots to help when you just felt overwhelmed by stuff. People like Dr. Cee to offer help to every kid who needed it . . .

It was too different from what she'd known. She couldn't picture it.

Sor was looking directly at her. "Believe it, Sharon," he said softly. "The future works."

"And that should give you hope," Dr. Cee said.

"Why should it give me hope?" Jason demanded. "I don't live in your future. I got to go back to New York tonight, don't I? My New York's got its share of violence and disease, and then some!"

Dr. Cee said, "Don't you want to go back? Would you rather stay here?"

Jason was silent for a long minute. Finally he said, "No. My family's there, and my buds . . . I want to go back. But why you showing me the good times I can never have?"

Dr. Cee said, "Because you're going to help create them. You, too, Sharon."

Jason did a double take. Sharon sat very still. Dr. Cee said, "You don't believe me. But it's true. Remember when I said that a group of ten thousand heroes would save civilization in the next century? Well, we've had a few centuries since then to use sophisticated computer techniques to discover exactly who they were. Come with me; I want to show you something."

She led them across the park into a low colonnade, with a roof but no walls. Inside grew more genemod flowers. No, they weren't flowers . . . they were some sort of computer hardware, with tiny screens inside cups of stalks. No, the cups and stalks *were* flowers . . .

"They're both," Dr. Cee said. "Living plants, but they're also programmable. Listen."

As the Yanks entered the colonnade, the plants began to sing softly, music barely audible but so lovely Sharon stood transfixed. At the same time the flowers began to display names on their petals, in their flowery hearts, holding each lovingly for a few long moments. Sharon gasped.

"It said . . . it said . . ."

"That's right," Sor said. " 'Rose-of-Sharon Myers.' And 'Jason William Ramsay.' "

Dr. Cee added, "You're both among the Ten Thousand Heroes. Or will be when you grow up. Didn't you wonder why you two particular kids were yanked? And you, Robbie and Jofrid, the data banks record that in your own times, you will also make a significant difference for the better."

That brought Sharon up short. Robbie, make a difference for the better? He had grit, sure, and he had helped the Yanks mission to succeed . . . but he was also a thief, a killer of small animals, a liar and cheat . . . Suddenly Sharon didn't believe in the Ten Thousand Heroes at all. She herself wasn't a hero type. Why, until she came to Jump, she was hardly brave enough to open her mouth in public.

Once again, Dr. Cee seemed to know what Sharon was thinking. Dr. Cee said, "Grit isn't fearlessness, Sharon. And it isn't insisting other people do what you want. Grit is finding other ways to get something done even when people refuse to cooperate with you. It isn't pushing other people around. Instead, it's not giving up, even if you have to try twenty-eight different plans before one works. It's persistence in the face of fear."

Sharon didn't answer. She felt too embarrassed to answer. Even Jason looked a little embarrassed at seeing his own name among the Ten Thousand Heroes. Did he believe it was true? Sharon couldn't tell. All Jason said was, "Coach Patterson wouldn't ever believe *this*."

"Well," Dr. Cee said, "people don't always—"

"Look!" Robbie suddenly yelled. "Metal guv'nor!"

And then Robbie was sprinting across the park, yelling and laughing. Sharon saw a robot rushing toward the small nineteenth-century kid. The robot *looked* like da Vinci—it was da Vinci! Even his voice sounded the same when the others rushed close enough to hear it. Robbie had thrown his arms around the 'bot and hugged him—*Robbie*, who never let anyone touch him except in a fight!

"Metal guv'nor, Robbie thought you was dead!"

"No, no, merely temporarily inactive," da

Vinci said. "But now I'm retrofitted and upgraded. Our plan with the Panurish and the gambling game worked, I'm told."

"Bang up to the echo!" Robbie said. His sunny smile was back. He looked, Sharon thought, like himself again. "And you know what, metal guv'nor? This lady says Robbie's going to be a bleedin' hero when I grow up!"

"The historical data banks confirm it," da Vinci said.

"I never would!" Robbie said. "But long as you're not dead, metal guv'nor, it don't matter. Right as rain, Robbie is."

Sor said, "You have more good in you than I once thought, Robbie."

Jofrid said, "If Dr. Cee had a dream about the future, you should listen, Robbie. Dreams are sometimes powerful messages."

Jason said, "Welcome back, da Vinci. How you doin'?"

Sharon said nothing. But she looked around her: at the beautiful, peaceful city. At the contented, productive people. At the colonnade of the Ten Thousand Heroes.

She still didn't believe she would be one of them. But another belief was growing in her. Despite her mother, despite Johnna, despite the meanness and selfishness she saw every day in Spencerville, Sharon had a thought she'd never thought before, and would once have believed to be stupid.

Maybe, she thought, maybe the future will be okay.

Maybe it will be wonderful.

21

"That was a great meal," Jason said. "*I* sure
pigged out. And on behalf of all the Yanks, we
want to say thank you before we say good-bye.
We know we got to go back to our own times
now, but I know we're all gonna be raving about
this great place to all our buds back there for a
real long time."

Every single adult face at the table went rigid.
Now what did I say? Jason though. His speech
was going so good! The Yanks and the Jump
kids and the seven scientists on the project had
been really into the party, eating and talking
and laughing. Then Dr. Cee asked Jason to "say
a few words" before Dr. Orgel spoke. So Jason
did. And now everybody looked like he'd slapped
them with a dead fish.

He tried again. "I know that when I'm back
in New York, I'm going say nothing but good
things about all you guys. I'll tell everybody that
2336 really has its act together, and it was, like,
my privilege to help you guys out with the Panurish."

More silence. Dr. Orgel was scowling like a

major thunderstorm. The other scientists, even Dr. Cee, looked unhappy.

Finally she said, "Jason, we thought you understood that . . . Didn't you run the program da Vinci gave you after we got back from the tour of Edge Station? Remember, he gave everybody a communication cube to listen to?"

"Well, yeah, he did that. But I didn't exactly have time to play it, what with one thing and another." The truth was, he'd taken a nap instead. He'd really needed some zzzzz's. "What did it say?"

Sor answered for Dr. Cee. "It said you won't remember anything about your trip into the future."

"Come again?" Jason said, incredulous. Everybody else at the long table was either looking at Jason or glancing sideways at each other.

"I'm afraid it's true, Jason," Dr. Cee said. "You will undergo a selective-amnesia field before we return you to your own time. We return you within a few minutes of when you left, so nobody has time to miss you. And you remember nothing."

"*Why?* That's so cheesy!" Jason blurted. They weren't going to let him remember this major mission? That *he'd* led so successfully? They were going to take that away from him?

"Try to understand," Dr. Orgel said. "If you remember what happened to you, or if you aren't returned to the same few minutes we yanked you from, it could change the past. *Our* past. You might act in ways that are different from how history says you already acted. That could lead to a different future—but we live in *this* future. We can't risk losing it. In addition, our scientists think even worse things might result—damage to the fabric of time itself. So it's better if you don't remember what happened to you."

Jason considered. It made sense, but he still didn't like it. "You mean—not anything? I won't remember anything?"

Dr. Cee sighed. "We don't know for sure. We think the selective-amnesia field is one hundred percent effective, but we can't t-port back in time ourselves to check it out. Remember, Jason—all of you—we haven't been yanking kids for very long. These are new procedures."

Jason felt better. Maybe he would remember some of this.

"Well, then, if we won't remember this, we better do it right now, while we definitely got it. So I'm going to ask my fellow Yanks to each say a few words, too. Sharon, you first."

Sharon looked alarmed. "No, not me."

"Yeah, you," Jason said. "Chill, Sharon, it's no big deal. Just a few words."

Sharon stumbled to her feet at her place around the table. Jason could see her tremble slightly. She really was a shy babe. But she was all right.

"Th-thank you for bringing me here. And for treating Tara and me so well. And . . . and . . ."

She stopped. Jason thought she was too tongue-tied to say anything more. But she surprised him.

"And even though I won't remember you all, you'll be with me anyway. Like the poet Keats said,

" 'Heard melodies are sweet, but those unheard
Are sweeter.'

All of you will remain unheard melodies in my
heart." Sharon sat down. Everyone applauded.

Jason stood stunned. Who thought shy
Sharon could turn so eloquent? Aloud he said,
"Girl's got the gift of gab, all right. Jofrid?"

Jofrid stood. She wore her same green dress,
clean now, and her red-gold braids hung shining
over each shoulder. She said simply, "May the
gods smile on each of you. And should you travel
to Iceland, the hospitality of Langarfoss is open
to you all."

Jason led the applause, although he doubted
that he'd be going to 987 Iceland any time soon.
Did Jofrid even understand she'd been traveling
in time? It was hard to tell. "Robbie?"

Robbie stood, looking very small. Da Vinci sat
beside him. Robbie started to say something,
stopped. He looked at da Vinci, who said, "Yes,
Robbie. You must."

Robbie looked momentarily sad. Then he
pulled from his pocket the small folded computer on which Dr. Cee had drawn the nested-
cylinder diagram of Edge Station. Dr. Cee
gasped in surprise and felt her empty pocket,
where she had last put the computer. Robbie
laid it on the table. Next he pulled out a small
bag of tools that made Sor plunge his hand into
his own empty pocket. Next, a packet of Jofrid's
plant powders. Finally, Jason's wristwatch.

"Robbie gives 'em back," Robbie said. "To my
friends."

Nobody knew what to say.

Finally Jason said, "Good job, Robbie!" and applauded. Everyone else followed. Robbie smiled at them sunnily.

I still wouldn't trust him as far as I could throw him, Jason thought, but he had to laugh anyway. Robbie was Robbie. And he was a survivor. Jason retrieved his wristwatch.

"Sor, say a few words?"

Sor stood. After Robbie, he looked tall and healthy and handsome. *I'd play him on center guard*, Jason thought. *A natural.*

"I wasn't yanked from a different time for this mission," Sor said, "and unlike the others, I hadn't demonstrated grit in the past. But I'm grateful I got to meet those who did, and to work with them, and to learn that I, too, could make a contribution. To quote Jason—we got it done!"

Sor got the loudest applause of all. *Yeah, you got grit*, Jason thought at him. Yet Sor gave others the credit. A dude worth knowing.

"And now Dr. Orgel with the big news," Jason said.

Dr. Orgel stood. To Jason he didn't look like a man with big news. He scowled—when didn't the man scowl? He was the only Gloomy Gus in 2336, seemed like. Oh, well. Always one.

"We on the Yanks project wish to extend our gratitude and thanks to everyone of you," Dr. Orgel said. "You've made a significant contribution to our understanding of the Gift Givers. I have three things to tell you. Before I do, however, let me repeat some background for our time visitors.

"You should remember that the Gift Givers arrived only six years ago. When they gave us the sally ports and t-ports, they promised yet more wonderful technology that would let us explore the universe in ways we can hardly dream of. But *only* if we first take the Nine Great Steps. We have already taken the First Step: to colonize our own solar system without destroying our homeworld. We think the Second Step is to show initiative about discovering what the Third Step is. And the Third Step may have been outlined for Captain Kenara by the Gift Givers who landed the *Discovery* just before all the adults on it died."

Jason looked at Mant. At Billin, Corio, Wu— all the Jump kids whose parents had died with Captain Kenara. They stared steadily at Dr. Orgel. Jason suddenly realized that they wanted to hear that their parents' deaths had at least accomplished something—that as a result, humanity was a bit closer to completing the Nine Steps. Well, Jason thought, if it were my mom that died, I'd want to know that, too. He found he was holding his breath to hear what Dr. Orgel would say next.

Dr. Orgel seemed to know how everyone felt. His voice softened from its usual harshness. "I said I had three things to tell you all. Here they are.

"First, the vase from the *Discovery* was indeed hastily painted with Morse code. Sharon was right. Captain Kenara chose Morse code so no aliens could easily steal information meant for humanity alone."

Jason whispered to her, "Way to go, Sharon." She blushed and smiled.

"Second," Dr. Orgel said, "we translated the

Morse code on the vase, using the arcane-language library stored in our data banks."

Dr. Orgel paused. Jason felt everyone in the room tense even more.

"Third, we know what Step Three is. It's this: We must share our own most advanced technology with at least one other alien race that is not more advanced than we are."

Jason's mind raced. Share their own most advanced technology! But . . . He called out, "Does it count as 'sharing' if the Panurish *stole* the advanced technology? They stole all that stuff from the *Discovery*!"

Corio called, "Are the Panurish more or less advanced than us?"

Sor said, "The technology the Panurish stole was six years old! Does that count as 'our most advanced technology' or not? We wouldn't let them get da Vinci's identity chip, which is more advanced!"

Everyone talked at once, calling out questions, arguing with neighbors. Dr. Cee held up her hand for quiet.

"We don't yet know the answers to these things. But we're going to study what we have, and try out various possibilities. Meanwhile, we wouldn't even know this much if it weren't for the Yanks and their true grit. So I'd like to propose a toast."

She stood and raised her glass. Everyone else did the same. "To the Yanks," Dr. Cee said. "May all the times of your life enrich you."

Good one, Jason thought. He laughed and raised his glass.

The Yanks stood in the time-port chamber beside Dr. Cee. Jason, Jofrid, Sharon, Robbie, Sor, da Vinci. They looked at each other. There were no words. But they could hug each other, and they did. Even Robbie.

Then four of them walked, one by one, through the time port and vanished.

Sharon shook her head. For just a minute she'd felt the weirdest sensation: a sort of tingling in her head, between her eyes. Then it was gone.

She stood on the glassed-in back porch, with Tara buttoned under her coat. What had she been about to do? Oh, yes—take Tara out for some air.

But that wouldn't solve her main problem. What was she going to do with Tara while she was in school all day?

Inside Sharon's coat, Tara started to struggle. The baby didn't like being held so close. Sharon loosened her coat and lifted Tara out. She set the baby on the porch floor, then sat down on a broken lawn chair to think. If she balanced carefully, the lawn chair wouldn't fall over. She'd been meaning to fix it, but she knew she wasn't very good at fixing things. She wasn't mechanical.

Mechanical. A sudden picture flashed in Sharon's mind: a mechanical man with long tentacles holding Tara. Weird! Where had that come from?

Grit isn't fearlessness, Sharon. It's not giving up, even if you have to try twenty-eight different plans before one works.

What on earth was that? Sharon's mouth made an O of pure astonishment. There'd been a voice in her head, a strange woman's voice . . . whose? What was happening to her?

She waited, but the voice didn't speak again. Instead, Sharon found herself thinking about her problem more calmly and clearly than she had before.

I need money so Mrs. Northrup will watch Tara.

I can't earn it at the library.

I'm not good at mechanical things.

What *am* I good at? Schoolwork. Homework. Organization. Taking care of small kids.

I could tutor younger children and earn more money than I could at the library. I know the material, and all my teachers would give me references.

Slowly Sharon got up from the lawn chair. She could do it. She could go down to the middle school and the elementary school and see if they had a tutoring program. If they didn't, maybe her old teachers could suggest names of kids who needed help.

She could do this. She was sure. Her plan would work.

And if it didn't—she'd think of another.

Tara, tired of crawling on the porch floor, held up her arms. Sharon picked up the baby. She opened the porch door and carried Tara down the steps, starting toward the elementary and middle schools. As she walked, Sharon found herself humming.

"Yo, bro. You gone deaf and dumb?"

Jason looked up. Brian stood beside him in front of the magazine rack. Outside the grocery store he could hear the traffic on Amsterdam Avenue, cabs honking and bus brakes hissing. "Hey, Brian. How you doin'?"

"How *you* doin'?" his brother retorted. "I come in here and find you standing like a zombie. You okay?"

"Sure," Jason answered. But actually he felt a little strange. Was he maybe coming down with a bug? But he didn't exactly feel sick either.

"Well, you gonna stand there all day, or we gonna go on home?"

"I'm right behind you," Jason said.

The brothers fell into step as they walked north on Amsterdam. Brian checked out the babes. Jason felt preoccupied—by what? He didn't know—until suddenly he stopped dead. "I know that girl!"

"Yeah? Which one?" Brian said interestedly.

"Across the street! In green!"

A small girl in a green skirt and top flagged down a cab. Shining red braids hung over her shoulders.

"No, wait, it's not her," Jason said.

"Who?"

"I don't know."

Brian peered at him. "You get whomped with the ball today, Jason?"

"No. No, I just thought . . . forget it."

The brothers walked on, Brian shooting small concerned glances at Jason. Finally Jason said, "Brian?"

"Yo."

"You know them exams on Saturday? At school?"

"The PSATs? Yeah, what about 'em?"

"I think I might take them after all. If I can still sign up. I been thinking I might . . ."

"Might what?"

"Might think about college in a few years. Maybe. If I don't, like, make it in pro ball."

Brian let out a long breath. "Good move, bro. You do it. You smart enough."

"I don't work hard, though. Coach says I don't work hard enough at anything."

Brian said, "But you can."

Jason considered. "Yeah, I can." He considered some more. "Yeah! I really can."

Jofrid blinked in the bright sunlight. What had she been doing? Oh, yes, bringing fresh water to the Hall, where visitors had just arrived. Men from the Allthing, they were, to see her father on some matter. And her mother had sent Jofrid for water. What ailed her, stopping on the way to daydream like this?

Bucket in hand, Jofrid hurried to the spring-house. The May afternoon was bright and warm at Langerfoss. Jofrid filled her bucket with sweet water and started back toward the homestead.

She heard a sound overhead and looked up. Four singing swans! A sign of good luck! Whatever the visitors had come for, it would bring good fortune to her father's homestead. Jofrid watched the swans until she could no longer hear their song. And yet, it seemed she could.

Heard melodies are sweet, but those unheard
Are sweeter; therefore, ye soft pipes, play on;
Not to the sensual ear but, more endeared,
Pipe to the spirit ditties of no tone.

Jofrid stopped so suddenly that a little water sloshed out of her bucket. How had that bit of a poem come into her head? She was no skald. And the poem sounded like no poem or saga she had ever heard a skald recite.

Mayhap she was going mad. Sometimes trolls, who could take any shape they chose, turned themselves into singing swans to drive a person mad.

But there was no time to worry about it now. Her mother waited for this water to add to the stew bubbling on the hearth. They would have two more mouths for dinner.

Jofrid carried the bucket into the Hall, careful not to spill any more. From the High Seat her father called out to her. "Dottir, come here."

Jofrid exchanged looks with her mother. It was unusual for her father to summon any woman to the High Seat, let alone his most willful and rebellious daughter. He disliked the idea that she might disgrace him by talking back and appearing too bold. Yet now he was summoning her in front of visitors!

"Yes, father," Jofrid said. She approached the High Seat. She should keep her eyes cast down, of course, but she couldn't help taking sideways peeps at the visitors.

Her father noticed. He scowled at her. "This is my girl, Kettil. As I have said, I wish I could say she is obedient and maidenly, but I cannot. She was handfast to Thorfinn Egilson, but he told me this very day that he wishes to break the handfast because of Jofrid's sharp tongue. He says he does not want a wife who will talk back to him and dispute him. However, I can vow that while Jofrid may be outspoken, she at least is quick and skilled at all of woman's art. She can cook and spin and weave and nurse."

Two men stood with her father. The older, a richly dressed homesteader, inspected Jofrid as if she were a horse he might want to buy.

"A pretty girl, Sigurd. I have heard of her willfulness, however. But my Erik saw her at market, and at the Allthing last summer, and he insists on asking for her."

Jofrid's head flew up. Asking for her! That meant this man's son wanted to marry her . . . Why? Who was he?

Her eyes met those of the young man standing beside his father. She didn't remember seeing him at market or at Allthing. Erik Kettilson stood a head taller than Jofrid. He was handsome, she thought, with curly dark hair. For just a moment he reminded her of somebody, but she couldn't think who. The moment passed.

The young man caught her staring at him, which of course she should not do, and smiled at her. But he addressed her father.

"Sigurd Aronson, I like a woman who knows her own mind. Who will speak out frankly with me, that we may have conversation in my homestead. Who will work and plan beside me, that we may prosper together. I think Jofrid is such a woman. I ask you for her."

Her father said, "Your father and I have discussed the dowry, and come to an agreement. You have my permission to be handfast to Jofrid."

Jofrid knew that no one would ask *her* permission. But if they had, she might have been inclined to give it. She liked what this Erik Kettilson said about working and planning side by side. And if he really liked a woman who spoke her own mind . . .

Maybe the singing swans had been good luck after all. Or maybe it was the bit of poem that had come to her from nowhere. Another piece of it lay in her mind yet . . . *A flowery tale more sweetly than our rhyme* . . .

She lifted her chin and smiled at Erik Kettilson.

"Stop, thief! Stop him!"

Robbie dashed toward the London street, away from the shouting voice. Something lay in his hand—what? A bracelet, it was, snatched off a lady's wrist just moments ago—what lady? Where was he?

"Stop him! He's a thief!"

Robbie ran into the cobbled street, to escape

to the other side. He didn't see the gentleman who thrust a walking stick across his path to stop him. But he felt the cane trip him and he went down, already rolling, just as a chestnut mare harnessed to a tilbury came at a spanking pace over the cobblestones. The horse's hooves sliced the air above Robbie's head. A woman screamed.

Then Robbie was clear, having rolled through the plunging hooves, and was running down an alley on the opposite side of the street.

Lor', but that was close! Losing his touch, he was. One more fork like that and he'd be in the basket for sure, dead as Wallam's cock.

Robbie leaned against a cookshop and breathed hard for a few minutes. When he had his breath, he started back to Whitechapel, keeping a sharp eye out for the beadle. Wouldn't do to get caught now. Not when he had this little bauble. Old Joseph'd give him three pounds for it, easy.

By the time he sold the bracelet, it was almost sunset. Robbie loitered beside a tavern he knew, alongside the river. From inside came great shouts of laughter. But he didn't go in.

The way the river light shimmered on them cobblestones . . . it made a kind of mist, like. No, not a mist . . . something else. It looked like a . . . a . . .

Lor', what was wrong with him tonight! A body'd think he was bosky, and he hadn't never had a drop! But look at that river mist again . . . Look at it shimmer . . .

The sun set and the shimmer went away.

Still Robbie stayed outside the tavern, leaning on the railing by the river. Finally a larger boy passed him.

"Ned—you had some schoolin' once, ain't you? Can you read?"

"I can read," the older boy said. "What for, Robbie? T'ain't no help forking the gentry."

"I know," Robbie said. "But can you read that, then, Ned?" He pointed to a poster attached to the brick wall outside the tavern.

"You always was a rum lad, Robbie," Ned said. But he read the poster aloud:

LECTURE

**The Public Is Cordially Invited To Hear
At the Royal Institute
On June 30 at Seven O'clock
Dr. William Herschel, Astronomer
Discoverer of the Planet Uranus
Speak on
"The Future of the Astronomical Sciences"**

"Uranus," Robbie said. And then, all at once in a little explosion he didn't know was going to happen, "Neptune!"

"What?" Ned said.

"Neptune. Sally port."

"Don't know no Sally Port, only old Sally Wutherspoon over to the Boar and Crown," Ned said. "You be a rum lad, Robbie. Always was." Ned went inside the tavern.

Robbie stood still. He had no idea what those

words meant: "Neptune." "Sally port." And that shimmer off of the river . . .

Robbie shook his head. He must have a touch of fever. Be all right tomorrow, he would.

Still—he might just go hear this astronomer cove, this Dr. Herschel, talk about the future. You never knew, did you. Might be something interesting there.

Just might be.

New York Times bestselling author

DAVID BRIN'S

OUT OF TIME

continues in July 1999 with

TIGER IN THE SKY

BY SHEILA FINCH

In the year 2345, young heroes have been yanked from 1999 to battle an alien menace. Soon they must seek help from the more distant past....Tough-minded Nan and brainy Jerry find themselves yanked into the future to join "team members" Ailee, from 2234, and Will, from 1579, on a mission to Oort One. The base is overrun with alien pests that cause mysterious electrical disturbances and threaten the station's very life support systems. The Thogs are furry, they're cute, they're no bigger than gerbils, and they're breeding like crazy. They might seem harmless, but with their strange mental effect on humans, they have the power to destroy everything—even the Earth itself—unless the team's final desperate plan turns out to be the cat's meow...

FREE! FREE! FREE!

DAVID BRIN'S

OUT OF TIME

P O S T E R   O F F E R

Avon Books is pleased you've chosen the exciting new **OUT OF TIME** series by *New York Times* bestselling author **DAVID BRIN** and a team of highly acclaimed science fiction writers. As our welcome gift to you, we'd like to send you a dynamic full color poster illustrating this original science fiction adventure series—absolutely FREE! Just fill out the coupon below, and send it to us with proof of purchase (sales receipts) of: *Yanked* (on sale in June 1999), *Tiger in the Sky* (on sale in July 1999), and *The Game of Worlds* (on sale in August 1999) and we'll rush a poster your way.

Void where prohibited by law.

- -

Mail to:
Avon Books, Dept. BP, P.O. Box 767, Dresden, TN 38225

Name_____

Address_____

City_____

State/Zip_____